OOR HOOSE

OOR HOOSE

❊ ❊ ❊

JAMES BARCLAY

❊ ❊ ❊

LINDSAY PUBLICATIONS

First published in 2000 by
Lindsay Publications
Glasgow

© James Barclay 2000

ISBN 1 898169 25 X

British Library Cataloguing-in-Publication Data
A Catalogue record of this book is available
from the British Library

Designed and typeset by Eric Mitchell, Bishopbriggs, Glasgow
in Plantin 10 on 12 point
Cover illustration by John Gahagan, Glasgow

Printed and bound in Finland by WS Bookwell

CONTENTS

✷ ✷ ✷

ONE

▨ ▨ ▨

THE LADIES OF BLOTTO STREET, IN GLASGOW'S EAST END HAD petitioned the corporation to have it's name changed. It was not without a tremendous battle that the City Fathers decided to acquiesce . . . especially now that the local elections were coming up. So Blotto Street became Glenvernon Street. The name of the street may have changed but the character did not.

The ladies of the now newly-posh named street, continued to practice their daily ritual of 'Hingin' Oot The Windae'. To the dusty tenement dwellers their windows were the windows on the world. After the weans had been packed off to school, the messages done and the house tidied up, it was a case of 'oot the windae' and from there they could watch the world go by. They pummeled their cushions, folded their arms and poked the heads oot, each heavy chest resting snugly on its cushion.

At a certain time, on each side of the street, a head would appear from the aperture in the grey stonework. Looking lengthwise from end of the street, the scene resembled the cackle of battery hens.

Cloth-curlered heads bobbed and voices were raised to friends passing underneath.

"Rerr day, intit?" was one of the most frequent cries. "Is yer man workin' yet?" was another. "Ah'm jist watchin' for the coalman," was another. And the buzz went on for most of the day. It was a happy life for the ladies of Glenvernon Street and, although most of them had television sets and radio, most of their news was transmitted from the street below by "freen's".

The blow that was to shatter their lives came right out of the blue – a favourite colour in some of these parts

The offical letter was pushed through the letter boxes of the three-storey building at number twenty-seven. The shock news from the factor, Hector McNab, Esquire, senior partner in the

7

firm, McNab, McNab and O'Reilly. It informed tenants that the building was to be demolished and that all residents would be re-housed.

Many of the tenants welcomed the news – seeing a gleaming new home with a bathroom and inside toilet. But others were not happy about the enforced move.

It was 'the talk of the steamie' and windae voices became louder. Hector McNab, in person, had visited some of the tenants to reassure them that all would be well and that they would enjoy the change.

Bunty McGeachie and neighbour Senga Broon found themselves 'hingin' oot' their adjacent windows.

Bunty had removed her cloth curlers and replaced them with her electric rollers, purchased round the Barras by her man, Hughie, for her thirty-something birthday. Hughie was like that – all heart. Although the rollers were bought 'roon the Barras', Glasgow's famous street market, he swore to Bunty that they were brand new, although Bunty had detected some blonde hairs attached. But she didn't argue with Hughie, who might fly into a tantrum and pull the pulley down again. She said nothing but was proud to stick her head out of the window wearing her newly purchased crown.

"Hey, Senga," she cried, turning to her neighbour, " did ye get yer letter?"

"Who didnae!" Senga beamed, adding proudly, "Auld McNab came up an' visited me personally."

"Ah'm no' surprised," Bunty said, "He'd jist want tae take doon yer particulars – or anythin' else the dirty auld swine."

Moustachioed and tubby, McNab had a reputation for having octopusic hands when in the presence of ladies. Especially those who could not afford "key money" in their search for a house.

"Aye, well he got naewhere wi' me," Senga said, tightening her lips. "He says the buildin's comin' doon," she added.

"An' whit did *you* say?" Bunty asked.

Senga narrowed her lips even tighter. "Ah said, 'Aye, an' that's a' that's comin' doon'." Senga was pleased with herself.

Bunty smiled. "An' whit did *he* say?" she asked eagerly.

"He said that whitever hoose he allocates me depended on this interview," Senga grimaced.

8

"An' whit did *you* say?" Bunty said, shuffling on her cushion.

"Ah said, 'Get oan yer bike, ya dirty wee nyaff," Senga said with the sound of authority.

"An' whit did *he* say?" Bunty asked, all ears.

"He said, 'Well, ye had yer chance'," Senga replied.

"And whit did *you* say?" Bunty asked in anticipation.

"Ah said, 'Aye, an' that's mair than you got'," Senga said chuckling.

Bunty sighed. "He came tae see me, tae, but didnae try nothin'. He knew better."

Senga nodded, "Aye, well he probably knew the reputation your Sammy's got cos' he's never oot o' the Royal Infirmary's Casualty Department because o' the batterin' you gie 'im."

It was true. Bunty was known to give her diminutive husband, a good hiding now and then, particularly, on a Friday night, when he had dipped into his pay poke before handing it over to Bunty's outstretched hand.

Bunty screwed up her face. "Ah don't like a broken pey, Senga," she said adamantly, "Hughie should know by this time, gie me a broken pey an' you get a broken heid."

Senga nodded. "Aye, quite right, Bunty, So, wher are ye goin'?"

"Aw, ah've knocked it aff, Senga," Bunty replied, a water-melon smile on her face.

"Hughie's heid?" Senga asked worriedly.

"Naw, ma new location," Bunty said excitedly, "and Ah didnae need for tae dae anythin' tae please McNab," she added.

"So, wher are ye goin'?" Senga said curiously.

Bunty sighed deeply, "Ah am goin' tae Drum-Shapel," she said proudly. The huge Glasgow housing scheme, in the West of the city had already taken thousands of its citizens in the big reorganising of the city housing after the war. "Whit aboot you?" Bunty added, hoping Senga would be up the same close.

Senga shook her head. "Nae such luck," she said, downcast. "Ah had tae turn doon ma oaffer."

"Where were ye oaffered?" Bunty asked, curiously.

"Priesthill," Senga said, referring to a scheme south of the river Clyde.

"Ah heard that's a lovely scheme," Bunty, surprised that her neighbour had turned it down.

Senga shook her head. "Well, ma Wullie nearly did his nut when he heard where they wanted for tae put us. He couldnae even find it in his heart for to say Priesthill. Well, Ah mean he is a high heid yin in the Orange Ludge. His face turned blue when Ah telt him where they wanted tae put us."

"Well, at least his face went the right colour tae suit 'im," Bunty said."It's jist too bad there's no' a place called 'Billyhill'. Anywey, Ah saw auld McNab goin' intae Wee Maisie's hoose an' he was in there for mair than two 'oors."

The inuendo was not lost on Senga. "An' where is Wee Maisie goin'?" Senga asked, with a slight sneer.

"Newton Mearns," Bunty replied, clicking her tongue.

Newton Mearns was situated on the south side of the city. But it could have been a million miles away from most of the tenants in Glenvernon Street. The affluent area could have been on the moon for all they cared.

Bunty was in full stride. "Ah canny wait tae see him goin' in tae Big Jessie's hoose," she said, "There's mair men go in an' oot o' that hoose that go in an' oot of the gents' lavvy at Queen Street station."

"Where dae ye think she'll get allocated?" Senga said.

"Buckingham Palace," Bunty said cheekily.

"So, where ur ye goin', Senga?" Bunty asked.

"London Road," Senga said, "it's neutral and near Wullie's maw."

"Where does she stey?" Bunty asked, wondering why Senga wanted to live near her mother-in-law.

"She's buried in Dalbeth," Senga said, referring to the cemetery in the London Road.

Bunty smiled. "Aw, that's nice, so it is," she said, "Wullie's fond o' his auld mother?"

"Naw, it's no' that," Senga said, "He' s growin' totties on tap o' her grave. He tried for tae get an allotment but couldnae. So, he didnae see why he shouldnae use his maw's grave. Ah know it's unusual," Senga went on, "an' people have flooers on tap o' their loved wans graves. But they jist wither. Wullie's maw's got totties on tap o' her and we hiv chips every night.

It's a case of a chip aff the old maw – women's lib, y'see."

Bunty saw the sense in it and nodded. "Aye, well, as faur as Ah know everybody up this close wull be movin' oot soon. Everybody, that is, except the McPhatters. They're determined no' tae move oot, They've been up his close since they got married forty years ago."

Senga nodded, "Aye, Ah heard it was their Ruby Weddin' anniversary comin' up – nice, intit?"

Bunty nodded. "Aye, it's hard tae believe that Sadie an' Harry have been married forty years.

"Aye, Sadie looks that . . ." Senga began.

"Young?" Bunty interrupted.

"Haggard," Senga said snidely.

"It's a shame gettin' slung oot the hoose that's been yer life an' jist when ye're Ruby Weddin' Anniversary's comin' up," Bunty said, "Ah was lookin' forward tae seein' a' they flooers gettin' cerried up the close frae a' their freen's, so Ah was."

Senga grinned "It would be a chinge frae seein' Harry gettin' cerried up the close," she said, then, with a deep sigh, added, "Ah, well, Ah'd better get in an' make Wullie's supper."

Always interested in her neighbour's gastronomic prowess, Bunty inquired. "Whit are ye gien' 'im?"

"Mince," Senga said sharply.

"Ah thought your Wullie was partial tae lamb chops," Bunty said, "Has he loast his appetite?"

"Naw, he's loast his teeth," Senga snapped

"Aye, weel ye'd better get in right enough," Bunty agreed, "or you'll be losin' yours, if Ah know your Wullie."

"He widnae dare!" Senga said, narrowing her eye, "he'd get nae mair love bites."

Bunty let out a scream." You still gie Wullie love bite's?" she said incredulously.

"Depends," Senga said, "At night, when he climbs intae bed, if he sees ma wallies in a tumbler at the side o' the bed, he knows he's no' in fur a night of passion. But, if the gless is empty, look out Wullie!"

Bunty bellowed with laughter. "Aye, well, keep smilin'," Bunty said, "See ye the morra. Ah still canny get Sadie an' Harry oot o' ma mind," she added sadly. Whit's gonny happen tae them?"

11

"Time wull tell, Bunty," Senga said, "An' Ah should know plenty aboot time Wullie's done plenty o' it."

They laughed before retreating into their homes. But it was a hollow laugh.

* * *

Sadie McPhatter pulled the curtain aside from her window and heard the removal van's engine splutter as it coughed into life and slowly move away from the close mouth.

Number twenty-seven Glenvernon Street would never be the same again. For with that van the life and soul of that dusty tenement in Glasgow's east end had breathed its last gasp. The last family had gone and with it the laughter and tears that had echoed over a lifetime down the spotlessly clean stairs – the last family all but one. The news that the building was due for demolition had arrived in a brown envelope just months before. There would be no appeal. The eleven families – three in each of the three landings and two in the close itself, were offered new houses. To some, especially those with young children, the thought of a bathroom and inside toilet was a godsend. After years of having to use the stairhead lavatory, which more often than not, was occupied as you shivered, shuffling into the chill of the evening and in frustration and desperation going back into the house listening intently for the pull of the chain announcing its vacation, this would be *Shangri La*.

To Sadie that was no real compensation for the death of the building where everybody knew everybody 'up the close'. Where there was always a helping hand. Where one's suffering was everybodys pain. Where behind each door lived a midwife, a lawyer, a doctor and a plumber – without a certficate of approval on any of their walls. Certificates didn't matter, the smile and the need to help was more important than any fancy piece of paper. They were all graduates of Life's University.

Many of the families had gone to the new multi-storey buildings, later to be called high-rise flats, springing up. To Sadie, the ubiquitous *Towerin' Infernals* were an eyesore and nothing would tempt her to move into one.

12

Her husband Harry, agreed and when the postman brought the news of the impending demolition of the building. – their *home* – it was immediately despatched to the embers in the tiled interior fireplace. Three more offers of a house had arrived but each one was turned down by Sadie with Harry's backing. Threats of eviction from Mr Hector McNab, the pompous factor for the building had come and had been ignored

Harry and Sadie were now the sole occupiers of twenty-seven Glenvernon Street. Gone was the happy laughter of the children, the loud clatter of of hurrying boots racing up the stairs. The cries of '*O-PEN, Pee-En*' from the weans. The yelling of the coalman, humping a hundredweight on his back as though it were a bag of feathers. The scrubbing of the stairs with their lovingly laid white pipe-clay borders.

Only the McPhatters were left to bring a pulse to the almost derelict building. But for how long? The postman had long since stopped coming.

Harry and Sadie had spent their entire married life at number twenty-seven. Now in their sixties they had decided that their roots were too deeply imbedded They had raised their family in this house and there were too many memories – too many *happy* memories for them to leave without a fight.

Sadie saw the removal van give out a large belch from its exhaust pipe and vanish round the corner. She let the curtain fall back into place and crossing the room, sighed as she flopped on to the old easy-chair by the burning coal fire. She let her head rest back and closed her eyes.

She remembered how wonderful she felt when she was given the house after handing over a sweetner to the factor. Confetti was still dropping from her hat's veil as Harry carried her over the threshold. They had come straight from the Bridgeton Public Halls, in London Road, directly after the wedding reception. Harry was then working in Singers', in Clydebank. A job he was to keep until his retirement. His presentation gold-plated pocket-watch was still keeping good time and it was with some pride he pulled it from his waistcoat pocket and glanced at it when in company – even when he didn't want to know the time.

Their two children, Norman and Maggie, were born in that

house with old Mrs Goldberg, from up the stairs, in full attendance. Sadie remembered how, on the eve of his first Holy Communion, she stood an excited Norman in the zinc bath in front of the fire only to notice the red spots of measles covering his back. A disappointed little boy was put to bed and missed his big day. As expected, Maggie was to follow almost immediately. Sadie nursed them through all the other children's illnesses. This would not be just a house she would be leaving. This was a life. Like a recording machine, every wall held a voice, a laugh, a song and a cry.

Sadie sighed more deeply. Now in her old age and about to be evicted. She wondered where it would all end? It was forty years to the day when Harry carried her through that door. Her Ruby Wedding anniversary had come upon her suddenly and the passing years had come and gone mercilessly.

Sadie found herself drifting into sleep. Somewhere in the distance she could hear the radio playing Frank Sinatra singing 'Love and Marriage'. She smiled in her slumber only to be startled by Harry's voice booming.

"Hey, Sadie . . . waken up. D'ye forget whit day this is?"

Sadie sleepily rubbed her eyes. "Er . . . er . . . whi . . . whit is it, Frankie?" she stammered.

"*Frankie*?" Harry cried, "Frankie who?

Sadie, shaking off her drowsiness, laughed. "Ah was dreamin' aboot Frankie, there," she said.

"No' Wee Frankie Smellie?" Harry said. "

Sadie shook her head and chuckled. "Naw, don't be daft," she said, more in rebuke.

"Ah should hope no'," Harry said, "Ye widnae want tae be married tae him when ye've got a hunk like me."

"How no'?" Sadie said, "He's always loaded."

"Who wants tae be married tae a perpetual drunk?" Harry said, "stick wi' me, hen. Ah'm just a part-time drunk."

Frankie Smellie had been an old beau of Sadie's who worked for a perfume manufacturers. He was once a dwarf but had decided to give it up. Harry. who was trying to woo Sadie at that time, had an obsession about Frankie. He couldn't understand what Sadie saw in him and, when he would meet her in the street he would accuse her of going to meet him despite her denials. But Harry was no fool, Sadie wasn't carrying that small stool with her for nothing. He grew to hate Frankie Smellie and would show it sarcastically every time he passed Sadie in the street by sticking a clothes peg on his nose.

But now, on their Ruby Wedding Anniversary, he was stunned to hear Sadie mention Frankie's name again.

"Ah was dreamin' of Frankie Sinatra," Sadie snapped, reading his mind. "He was singin' oan the wireless durin' ma dream," she added, in way of mitigation.

Frankie Smellie was forced to leave his position with the perfume company because the managing director Oscar Stink, thought that Frankie's name was an embarrassment to the firm.

Sadie had not seen him for years and Frankie was now in a more lucrative position. Harry had met up with him a couple of times but Frankie Smellie had never mentioned Sadie during these frosty encounters, knowing full well that Harry, always a jealous man, would flatten him. Now Harry wondered if Sadie had really been dreaming of Frankie Sinatra or was covering up with maybe a memory from the past? He put the thought from his head but decided to get rid of all his Frank Sinatra tapes and replace them with something that would get rid of any tempting memories. He would later visit The Barras, Glasgow's famous street market and replace them with an old piano which was riddled with woodworm. There was nothing to beat home entertainment, he reckoned.

"Ye wurnae really thinkin' aboot Frankie Smellie, were ye?" he asked, reassuring himself.

"Don't be daft," Sadie said, flattered that Harry still had his jealous streak.

"Besides," Harry said, "who wants a man that takes his work hame wi' him?"

"Whit does he dae noo?" Sadie asked.

"He's an undertaker," Harry said.

Sadie's eyebrows shot up. She couldn't envisage Frankie in a tile hat. He'd always been afraid of death and once, when introduced to a woman at an orgy, was horrified to discover later that she was an undertaker. For two weeks after that he stood with his hand in basin of dettol.

Sadie finally said, "Ah don't believe it."

15

"It's true," Harry said, adding "When was the last time you saw Frankie?"

Sadie put her index finger to her cheek and thought. Finally, snapping her fingers, she exclaimed, "It was on television. He was in *Stars In Their Eyes,* Ah mind noo. He was in a group called *The Halleluja Brothers* gospel singers."

"Did they win?" Harry asked, trying to show interest

Sadie shook her head. "Naw, they came in twenty second and that no' only surprised them but surprised everybody else.

"How? Were they that good?" Harry said.

"Naw. there was only eighteen acts in it," Sadie replied.

Harry shrugged. "Well, they couldnae have got anywhere in show-business. Ah've never heard o 'The Halleluja Brothers'.

"Ah'm no' surprised," Sadie said, "they developed bad breath an' chinged their name tae The Halitosis Brothers."

Harry grimaced. He used to be a nine-stone weakling who suffered from severe halitosis and who ate four packets of extra strong mints a day to combat it. but ended up a twenty-six stone sumo wrestler with a breath that could ignite a Bunsen Burner.

"Aye, well, Ah'd rather ye dreamed aboot Frank Sinatra, hen," Harry said, "but it's *me* ye should be dreamin' aboot. Remember whit day it is." he added huffily

Sadie smiled and kissed him tenderly on the cheek. "Of coorse Ah remember," she said, "Forty years we've been merried, forty years," she repeated," it's oor Ruby Weddin' it reminds me o' the Good book."

Harry's eyebrows shot up. "Auld Moore's Almanac?" he said, puzzled.

"Naw," Sadie shook her head " the Good Book – the Bible."

"Oor weddin' anniversary reminds ye o' the bible?" Harry said, incredulously.

Sadie nodded."Aye, Moses," she said.

"Ah remind ye o' Moses?" Harry said, his eyes narrowing.

"Naw, his forty years in the wilderness," Sadie said."Jist like us."

Harry could not digest this revelation. "Imagine sayin' Ah remind ye o' Moses," he mutttered.

"Harry, "Sadie went on, "When Moses struck that rock wi' his

16

pole watter gushed oot, If you had been Moses Lanny would've gushed oot. You would've had the Israelites staggerin' aboot the wilderness for forty years."

Harry was hurt. "Aw, c'mon, Sadie," he said, "admit it Ah'm the light o' your life, int Ah?"

"So ye are, Harry, so ye are," she said, smiling.

Harry puffed out his chst. "Wan hundred watts, that's me," he said proudly,"A bright neon in yer life, a brightness for to envelope you, ma wee lamb."

Sadie's hand came up to her mouth as she hid a smile. "Oh, Ah thought ye said a *blight* in ma life," she said.

"Aw, ye don't mean that – dae ye?" Harry said, crestfallen.

Sadie patted his arm. "Naw, son, we've had no' a bad life, a' things considered."

"Aye, forty years, eh?" Harry said with pride, "Forty years o' hard work – makin' this wee hoose intae a *home* – gettin' the furniture, paperin' the wa's, layin' the linoleum, puttin' up the televison aerial – makin' this place whit it is today, aye it took a loat o' elbow grease, hen."

"Wan o' us had tae dae it," Sadie said flatly.

"Ye did a rerr joab," Harry said, proud of his wife, "So good, Ah was very nearly puttin' a cerd in the coarner shoap windae, hirin' ye oot."

"Aye, ye would've done tae – if ye could write," Sadie said cheekily.

"Harry laughed. "Aye, well as long as Ah know how tae write ma name." he said, "Ah can put ma 'X' doon a'right."

"Four X, ye mean," Sadie laughed. Then, seriously, "Still," she said quietly, "ye could always sign yer name tae a birthday card or a Christmas card, Harry, an' yer 'X's' were kisses. Oor weans never wanted . . . oor weans . . ." Sadie had a faraway look.

Harry put his arm around his wife's shoulder. He knew how Sadie missed Maggie and Norman. He did too. They were now in Canada – albeit by error. They had gone down to the Broomielaw with the intention of going on a day trip *Doon The Watter* to Rothesay and had boarded the wrong boat. A postcard had arrived six years ago from Toronto and that was their last communication. Sadie worried over them, especially

17

Norman whose short sightedness had always been a worry. Harry wondered how he was getting on in Canada. Did he manage to find employment as a football referee for example? He remembered the first day Sadie voiced her concern about Norman's short sightedness. He was just a schoolboy then. He had rushed excitedly into the house saying he had found a stray dog and begged to be allowed to bring it home. Sadie had finally condescended. But her first suspicions were aroused when he walked in with a horse – a Clydesdale. Fierce arguments ensued and Norman broke his heart when ordered to get rid of the nag as Sadie cried "We've nae room for it".

Harry smiled to himself as he thought of Maggie and Norman. He shuddered a little, too. "Aye, Maggie an' Norman they were the ugliest weans in the street."

Sadie's brows shot up. "Whit dae ye mean by that?" she snapped. "Oor weans wur not wan bit ugly."

"Naw, they was two bits," Harry said snidely.

"Remember Maggie came in second in that contest at Butlins. She won a cup." Sadie protested.

"Aye, Sadie," Harry said, "First was an alsatian."

"Well, it's no' every lassie that can say she won a cup at Butlins," Sadie retorted.

"It wisnae a cup, Sadie," Harry said, "It was a bowl filled wi' Bounce."

Sadie turned on him. "Oor weans were *not* ugly," she snapped then, after a pause, added, "Except that Maggie had a wee turn in her eye."

"A wee turn in her eye?" Harry exploded, "Sadie," he went on, "Maggie was the only wean in the street that could see roon' coarners."

Sadie dabbed ger eyes. "Oh, don't let us talk aboot the weans," she whimpered. "Ah greet every time Ah think o' them.".

Harry nodded. "So dae Ah," he said, "Especially Norman. Let's think aboot happier things."

"Like the first time we met," Sadie smiled.

"Aye, in Barraland," Harry whooped, his mind going back to one of Glasgow's most popular dance halls – and that very special night all those years ago.

"Ah must admit Ah didnae fancy you when Ah first clapped eyes oan ye," he said.

Sadie shrugged. "Ah didnae fancy you either," she said huffily, "Especially you wi' that daft hat ye had oan"

"A lot o' boys wore hats in them days," Harry said, just a little hurt.

"No' bishop's mitres, they didnae," Sadie scoffed. "And, besides," she went on, "you *did* fancy me, so don't kid yersel'."

Sadie was correct but Harry thought he'd keep her going. "Whit makes ye think that?" he said.

"It was the war years remember? Things were hard tae get. You swaggered ower tae me, Ah thought ye were goin' tae ask me for a dance, instead ye oaffered me a biscuit."

"It was a dug biscuit," Harry said faceciously.

"You said Ah was beautiful," Sadie said, hurt.

"Ye kept flutterin' yer eyclashes an' flashin' yer teeth an' clicken them . . . that put me right aff, so it did," Harry said recalling their first encounter.

"Lots o' lassies like tae use their nice, white teeth an' click them tae attract a man," Sadie said authoritatively.

"No' as castanets, " Harry said.

"Ye's got tae admit, though," Sadie went on, ignoring Harry's sarcasm, "There were some smashin' dancers went tae Barraland."

Harry nodded. "Aye, right enough . . . and ye wurnae a no' a bad wee hoofer yersel'," he said.

Sadie received the compliment graciously. "Ah took that efter ma maw. She was a rerr wee dancer," she said proudly.

Harry's eyebrows shot up. "Auld Bowly Bella?" he cried

"Ma maw was not bowly," Sadie said in defence.

"No' bowly?" Harry said, throwing up his arms despairingly. "Sadie, ye could get the Peggy Spencer Formation Team daein' a tango through her legs. She was the ugliest wee wumman in Glesca. Oor weans take efter her."

Steam jetted out of Sadie's ears. "Ma maw," she snapped, "was *nut* ugly. She was a wonderful wee wumman – marvellous for her age, so she was. When we walked doon the street together people would stop an' turn. They just couldnae believe she was ma auld mother."

"They probably thought she was yer auld faither," Harry sniped.

"Ma maw," Sadie snapped angrily, "was a neat wee wumman."

"That's the wey she liked her whisky, right enough," Harry said coldly.

Sadie tried to stifle her anger. She knew Harry was just winding her up. What she didn't like about the banter was that he was enjoying it. "Have you nothin' good tae say aboot ma mammy?" she said at last.

"Aye, she's deid," Harry said with a straight face.

Sadie cooled down. She would never win this argument. Harry was in full stride. She decided to change the subject.

"Ah wonder if oor Norman and Maggie remember it's oor weddin' anniversary?" she said quietly.

"Who knows?" Harry said, nonchalantly, although, deep down felt hurt. He ached more for Sadie's sake but would never show his emotions.

"Ah think aboot them a' the time," Sadie said quietly. "Ah'll never forget that day. The two o' them went doon tae the Broomielaw for a wee day doon the watter an' that was the last we seen or heard o' them . . . till we got that postcerd frae Toronto. They'd got on the wrang boat." Sadie shook her head sadly.

Harry nodded. "Aye, instead o' gettin' on the *Queen Mary Two*, they got on the *Queen Mary Wan*."

"It a' biled doon tae Norman's short sightedness . That always worried me."

"Aye, right enough," Harry said, "The first inklin' Ah got was that time we took him doon tae London an' we got separated in Oxford Street, remember?"

Sadie nodded. "Oh aye, Ah was worried sick."

"Then Ah saw him staunin' hivin' a conversation in the street an' wondered whit he was on aboot. Ah asked him whit he thought he was daein'?

"Whit did he say?" Sadie asked

"He said he was askin' this auld man for directions," Harry said.

"Directions tae where?" Sadie asked, puzzled.

Harry screwed up his nose. "Ah don't know. He was staunin' talkin' tae a pillar boax. 'That's a post box ye're talkin' tae,' Ah telt him but he just shrugged an' said he thought it was a Chelsea Pensioner who'd forgot tae put his teeth in."

Their eyes met and Sadie saw the twinkle in Harry's eyes. They burst out laughing and Sadie, giving her husband an affectionate shove, said "Aw, ya midden! Ye had me goin' there." But she quickly turned serious.

"But Ah still worry aboot Norman – baith o' them. Dae ye think they remember that this is oor anniversary?"

"Ah'm sure they're thinkin' aboot us, hen," Harry said, giving Sadie's arm an affectionate squeeze.

She smiled. Harry was there! Harry, with all his faults, was always there. She thought of their plight. Eviction was staring them straight in the face.

"Ye know, Harry," she said, "Ah just don't know whit we're gonny dae if they force us oot. Would ye no' even consider the high-rise flats? Ah shudder as well when Ah think aboot goin' intae wan o' them."

Harry nodded. "Me tae," he said. "Ah mean Ah'm frightened o' heights masel'. Ah even took dizzy turns when Ah had that big verruca."

Their eyes met again and they burst out laughing. Harry was always good for a laugh and she never took seriously his bantering – although sometimes it got to her.

Sadie was stunned when her parents accepted a flat on the twenty-third floor of a high-rise flat. Her mother, who died and who was buried in a barrel because of her legs, had to be winched out of the window to a waiting hearse because the lift was out of order – again. She wondered, too, why her father had moved into the *Towering Infernal* She knew how he suffered from vertigo. She remembered the time when the family booked a holiday in Majorca. Of how he went berserk on the plane and had to be restrained by two of the stewards and six of the passengers. They finally had to strap him to the seat and bring down an oxygen mask. Not only was Sadie shocked at her father's behaviour. She was also very embarrassed. The plane hadn't taken off.

Now she was sure of one thing. Nothing would induce her to

move into the multi-storeys. She was pleased, too, that Harry was of a similar mind. She wondered what kind of house Norman or Maggie had found in Canada?

She was sorry to see all of her neighbours up the close leaving meekly and taking whatever was offered. Not all had moved into the high-rise flats. Some had gone into buildings in worse condition than the one they had left.

Others were more fortunate and had gone to much more affluent areas. They knew they were in richer pastures when they saw the change of vermin. They didn't have rats running around, they had mink!

When Norman and Maggie had vanished that awful day Sadie was ill with worry for many months. And when the postcard had arrived from Canada she did cartwheels up and down the street. A feat that brought dozens of nosy neighbours pulling their curtains aside. Norman had acquired a job on a ranch. It was an occupation he had always imagined himself in ever since seeing Gene Autrey on the silver screen of the *Arcadia* cinema, in London Road. It was with deep pride he told his mother that was now a cowpoke on the *Wee Specky Swine* ranch and loved looking after the chuck waggon and the cowhands who trailed the huge herd of near-sighted cows.

When Sadie received the news she immediately went down on her knees and thanked the Almighty. Besides she was already down on her knees scrubbing the linoleum. Harry, too, was delighted that his offspring were doing well and immediately got plastered. He would have got plastered anyway but he always felt better raising a glass in a toast.

To others the thought of leaving the old tenement was an act of cowardly desertion. This was Sadie and Harry's home. It was their oasis in a clumsy, dirty world. Sadie could turn a blind eye to the dampness, although, for the sake of the growing children, had often complained to the house factor.

But love overlooks everything. Blemishes vanish. To Sadie, twenty-seven Glenvernon Street, was *Shangri-la*. Buckingham Palace was second-rate. Her prayer and dream was that Norman and Maggie would grow up healthy. That Norman would find a nice girl to marry and settle down and that Maggie, who was as ugly as Norman, might become a nun or

22

meet a man with a kindly guide dog. Norman's near sightedness had kept him back. His great ambition was to be a police-
man and he once plucked up the courage to go down to the
Eastern Police station, in Tobago Street, to "join up" He came
out that day, his chest puffed up and wringing with pride. He
had been told to start work on the following Monday. And he
did – and became an apprentice painter and decorator. He had
gone into the premises next door to the police station by mistake. His new boss was very understanding and started him off
by giving him the local pillar boxes to paint. And that's why
many boxes in the area are painted blue.

Sadie and Harry sat down together on the easy chair. Sadie
bent over and stoked the fire with the heavy brass poker from
the companion set

She leaned back. "Y'know," she began, 'Ah wonder if they
high-rise flats are really as bad as everybody paints them?"

Harry's brows shot up in surprise. "Are you kiddin'?" he
snapped.

Sadie knew that she was trying to convince herself. She
grimaced."Yer auld faither as well as a' oor neighbours made
the big mistake o' givin' intae that wee nyaff Hector McNab in
acceptin' wan o' they tower blocks. Every time Ah turn doon yer
faither's street and see him hingin' oot the windae, ma heart
goes up tae ma mooth. Ah mean, he's on the twenty-third flair."
Harry was adamant.

Sadie sighed. "Ye must understaun', Harry," she said, "Auld
folk find it hard for tae chinge their ways. Ma Da' *always* hung
oot the windae, so he did."

"No' by his braces, he didnae. Ah mean there's bungee
jumpin' and there's bungee jumpin." Harry said, screwing up
his eyes.

"Well, when ye see him daein' that ye should humour him,"
Sadie said.

"Ye want me for tae staun' underneath his windae an', when
he comes doon, tell him a joke?" Harry said facetiously.

"Don't be daft!" Sadie exclaimed.

"Ah did, wance, try for tae deter him," Harry said, "Ah stood
under his windae and when he came doon tae the grun' Ah
grabbed him by the ankles and the next thing Ah knew Ah was

flyin' up alang wi' him. No' only that, when Ah passed a windae on the fourteenth flair a wumman stuck her heid oot and stuck a shammy in ma haun' an' asked me tae dae her windaes on the wey doon."

"Ach, ye're haverin'," Sadie said dismissively.

"He's dead lucky he hisnae been flattened," Harry groaned.

"Ah thought you didnae believe in luck," Sadie said.

"Ah don't," Harry said. "Look at that time Ah applied for a joab in that shoap that selt bathroom suites, in Argyle Street. Noo where was ma luck there, eh? Bad luck jist follows me," Harry shook his head despairingly.

"But ye got that joab," Sadie said.

"That's whit Ah mean," Harry said.

"Ah admit the joab didnae last long," Sadie went on, "ye got fired efter a week for usin' the executive toilet."

"Ah was gied permission for tae use the executive toilet," Harry protested.

"No' the wan in the front shoap display windae," Sadie snapped.

"Ach, well, we've stuck it a' oot, hen," Harry said, in way of consolation.

Sadie nodded. Harry was right. They had pulled together and got through. "So we have, Harry," she said. "If only we could hear frae Norman an' Maggie again," Sadie had a faraway look.

Harry nodded. Aye, right enough," he said patting her shoulder, "They might be ugly weans but they're *oor* weans."

Sadie had tried not not admit to herself that her offspring were ugly. But maybe Harry was more truthful to himself. "Dae ye really see oor Norman as ugly?" she said.

"Look, Sadie," Harry said, "Ah wance took oor Norman tae Calderpark Zoo and there was a class o' school weans being showed around and, before Ah knew it, they were queuein' up tae feed him a bun. Noo, that's ugly Sadie, that's ugly."

Sadie had to admit that Harry was right. She nodded. "Right enough", she said, "they specs o' his did nothin' for him. Whit dae you think?"

Harry screwed up his nose "Sadie," he began, "maist folk go tae Specsavers or Vision Express for their glesses. No' many go tae C.R. Smith."

"Ah wonder whit he's daein' noo?" Sadie said. "Ah wonder if he's merried tae some poor lassie whose vision of beauty is somebody like Quasimodo."

"Ye never know," Harry said.

"Remember wance he nearly got a girlfriend? We were a' excited when he telt us he was bringin' her up for tae introduce her tae us."

"Aye, Ah mind fine," Harry said, "It was St Valentine's Day an' we thought that was a good omen, mind?"

Sadie nodded. "Oh, aye, Ah mind fine."

Her mind went back. She had gone to the Co-op and bought the most attractive cake she could find. It had pink icing and was decorated by two iced hearts speared by a flaming arrow. She recalled how she spent the day tidying up the house and laying the table. Of how she placed the cutlery as etiquette dictated. She had retrieved the two brass candlesticks from an old kist underneath the bed valance and had purchased two pink candles from Woolworths. She lit the candles, stood back and surveyed her work and was well pleased. She put a Frank Sinatra record on the radiogram and sat nervously on the edge of her chair by the fire – and waited. She wondered what kind of girl had fallen for her Norman. Harry, too, wondered. He wondered, too, if there were any signs of mental illness in her family.

Sadie and Harry were now re-living that big moment in their lives. Harry complimented Sadie on the culinary skill she had shown. Sadie was pleased that Harry had noticed her efforts. She had laboured over what to serve Norman and his new girl at the table. She watched Harry cutting his toenails and immediately thought on pigs trotters. But decided against it when it occurred to her that Norman's girl might be Jewish. She had settled for a fish dish and had laid out for starters. Oysters Kilpatrick. followed by stuffed bream with jacket potatoes.

Norman had come rushing in and made straight for Harry, who was sitting smoking his pipe and reading his *Evening Times*. Norman planted a wet kiss on Harry's cheek. "Hello, maw," he said, beaming.

Harry vigorously rubbed his cheek. "Ah'm yer da'," he growled, "that's yer maw ower there pickin' her feet."

Norman kissed Sadie. "Hello, maw," he said without embarrassment.

Sadie returned the kiss and began to remove her son's jacket. "There ye are, son," she said, "yer buttons are supposed tae be at the front".

Norman laughed. "Bella has got me in a tizzy," he chuckled. "Ah just don't know whit Ah'm daein' at times."

"That's love, son," Sadie smiled, straighening his tie. "There, noo. Bella, is that yer girlfriends name, Norman?"

Norman nodded. "Aye, mammy, she was called efter a famous film star."

"Oh, who was that, son?" Sadie said.

"Bella Lugosi," Norman said without smiling.

Sadie puckered her brows and Harry coughed. "Well – er – where is this film star?" Sadie said at last.

"Aw, Bella's no' a film star, mammy," Norman said, shuffling his feet.

"We're baith lookin' forward tae meetin' her," Harry said.

"An' Ah'm dyin' for tae sit doon and have a wee blether wi' her," Sadie added.

"She's awfu' shy, mammy," Norman said, "In fact she's jist started talkn' tae her ain maw."

Harry looked up, removing his pipe. "She disnae need for tae be shy wi' us, son," he said. "Ah think it's aboot time yer mammy an' me were introduced."

"Aye, right enough," Sadie agreed.

Norman shrugged. "Oh, a'right. Mammy, this is ma Da' – Da', this is ma Mammy."

Sadie took a playful swipe at him. "Away ye go, ya galoot," she laughed. "We meant we should be introduced tae oor future daughter-in-law."

"Who's that, mammy?" Norman asked, puzzled.

"Bella, of coorse," Sadie said, glancing over at Harry who turned away.

Norman shuffled his feet again. Harry and Sadie could see he was embarrassed. This was his first girlfriend and a big moment for him.

Harry broke the silence. "Whit – er – whit does Bella dae, son?" had asked hesitantly.

"Oh, she does everythin'," Norman brightened up."She gets up and has her breakfast, puts her claes on, goes oot and' that – know whit Ah mean?"

"Ah think yer faither meant whit does she work at? Whit does she dae for a livin'?" Sadie said.

"Oh'!'", Norman said. "She – er – works in the circus that's in the Kelvin Hall the noo,"

"Oh, that's interesting!" Sadie said with just some wonderment.

"Unusual, eh?" Harry piped up.

Norman grinned. "She says she couldnae dae anythin' else," he said. "The circus has been her life. She says she started frae scratch."

"Is it a flea circus?" Harry asked

"Naw, naw, it's a real circus, wi' elephants an' that," Norman replied, just a little hurt.

"Is she oan the trapeze?" Sadie asked with interest.

"Naw, she disnae touch drugs," Norman said.

"Ah didnae mean that," Sadie said in exasperation."Ye said ye were bringin' her tae meet us the night. So, where is she?"

"She's staunin' in the close," Norman said.

"*In the close?*" Harry and Sadie said in unison.

"Aye – er – she's a bit shy, y'see," Norman said,a little embarrassed.

Sadie took him by the elbow and steered him towards the door. "Right, you get right oot there and bring her in here immediately," she snapped.

"Ah'll dae it," Norman said, "but if only if youse wull be tolerant."

"Tolerant?" Sadie said, drawing her brows down.

"Norman nodded. "Would youse mind very much if she went intae the cupboard?" he said.

"*The cupboard?*" Sadie and Harry cried.

"Ah telt ye she was shy," Norman said, "She finds it hard for tae talk tae people." Ah suppose she talks tae the animals," Harry said facetiously.

"Oh, aye," Norman said with pride, "she's right pally wi' a monkey."

"Ye shouldnae demean yersel' like that, son," Harry said.

"She just disnae like talkin' tae people. She hardly opens her mouth," Norman said.

"Ye've got a treasure there, son," Harry said, avoiding Sadie's glare.

"Does she speak tae you, Norman?" Sadie asked.

"Oh, aye," Norman cried. "She spoke tae me a fortnight ago,"

"A foartnight between words, eh?" Harry beamed, "Definitely twenty-four carat."

"Look, son," Sadie piped up, "Marriage is a partnership. Ye canny go through life wi' you goin' intae bed at night an' yer wife goin' intae the broom cupboard. It's no' normal."

"It is if she's a scrubber," Harry said.

Sadie gave Harry a look that sinks battleships. Taking Norman by the elbow, she steered him towards the door. "Away you oot there and bring Bella in," she commanded.

"Ye're a pal, Mammy," Norman said, "Ah'll try an' talk her oot o' goin' intae the cupboard if ye promise no' tae look at her."

"Aye, you dae that, son. Ah'll shout on her first so that she knows we're friendly," Sadie said.

"Thanks, Mammy," Norman said, pecking Sadie's cheek.

Sadie stuck her head out and called loudly, "Bella – Bella – come on in, hen. We're no' lookin'."

Norman brushed past his mother. "Ah'll get her," he said.

Sadie turned round. Harry was still puffing on his pipe and reading his paper. Harry was giving a *laid back* impression.

"Bella's comin'," Sadie said, not wanting Harry to look disinterested. Harry put the paper aside, spat on his hand and slicked his hair down.

They stood watching the door. Harry and Sadie were just a little excited. This was the day they had hoped for. The day they never dreamed would ever come. Norman had a girlfriend at last. All of Sadie's votive candles had paid off. She put her hands together, looked heavenwards and said a silent prayer of grateful thanks.

Norman entered the house first followed by Bella. Harry's mouth fell open the minute their eyes met. Sadie collapsed on the floor in a dead faint. Bella had the the most magnificent red beard that would have done justice to a young Santa Claus.

Norman and Harry rushed to Sadie's aid. Harry cradled his

wife's head in his arms. "Sadie – Sadie," he pleaded,"waken up.
– come on, noo."

Sadie did not stir. Nodding across the room, Harry said,
"The cupboard's ower there, hen."

Bella smiled.

"That's a'right, Mr McPhatter" she said, " Ah'll just sit doon
here, next tae yer comotose wife, just as long as ye don't look at
me."

Bella moved over and sat on the settee. She tutted and, shaking her head, looked down on the still body of Sadie.

Harry was worried that Sadie might come round and see
Bella staring down at her. He tapped Bella on the shoulder.

"Dae ye want a brown paper bag tae put ower yer heid?" he
asked, seriously.

Bella shook her head. "Naw, thanks," she said.

"It was jist so Ah widnae look at ye," Harry said in way of an
explanation. "Will Ah put wan ower *ma* heid? he added

Bella thought for a moment and then, shaking her head, said.
"Naw, but Ah hope that when Missus McPhatter comes tae, she
disnae want tae sit an' talk tae me.That would be hell, so it
would."

"Ah can understaun' that," Harry said.

Sadie gave a shudder, opened her eyes and sat bolt upright.
Turning, she saw Bella looking at her. Sadie brought the back
of her hand up to her forehead, gave a slight groan and collapsed once more into unconsciousness.

Harry took Norman gently by the arm and steered him aside.
"Are you sure ye know whit ye're daein', son?" he said.

Norman stared at him blankly. "Whit dae ye mean, Da'?" he
asked puzzled.

"Ah mean dae ye know whit ye're daein'? There's no' many
boys bring up their lassies and their maw's faint." Harry
snapped.

Norman shrugged. "Ah don't understaun' it," he said, "Ah fell
in love wi' Bella the first time Ah clapped eyes on her."

"Was she bendin' doon tyin' her lace at the time?" Harry said.

Norman shook his head. "Naw, she wears slip-ons, Da'."

Harry tried again. Have ye – er – no' noticed somethin'
different aboot her?, son?"

"Ah just know that she's got somethin' other lassies Ah've met hivnae got," Norman said with some pride.

"Ye can say that again," Harry said.

"Aye, that's ma Bella," Norman sighed,

"Ye agree, then, that Bella's got somethin' other lassies don't have, eh?" Harry said, hoping he was getting through to his son.

"Oh, aye, she has." Norman said, his chest inflating slightly.

"And whit dae ye think it is?" Harry asked, furrowing his eyebrows.

"*Me!*", Norman beamed.

Harry' shoulders sagged. "That's no' whit Ah meant, son," he said.

"Ah just know Ah love her," Norman went on, "and someday Ah'm gonny kiss her – maybe the morra. It's her birthday and it'll be a good excuse. Ah'll just get up the courage and go right up tae her and plant wan right on her lips."

"Ye'd be better plantin' *her*," Harry said out of the side of his mouth.

"Ah'll need tae buy her a present for her birthday but Ah canny think whit tae get her. Any ideas?" Norman asked with a pleading look.

"Whit aboot a Remington?" Harry said.

"Whit dae ye mean, Da'?" Norman asked.

"Look, Norman," Harry began, "Are *you* sure Bella's no' yer optician's daughter?"

A note of anger crept into Norman's voice. "Ah don't know whit ye're gettin' at, Da', It's ma Bella's birthday an' that' a' Ah've got on ma mind the noo. Ah was thinkin' o' buyin' her a fur coat but she's dead against cruelty tae animals. She's right intae this Animal Rights gemme. She walks, talks an' sleeps animals. She's always got oor furry creatures on her mind." Norman said.

"On her face as well," Harry said.

"Whir are you tryin' tae say, Da'?" Norman said with annoyance.

"Ah hate tae tell ye this, son," Harry said," But Bella's got a beard – a rid wan!"

"Are ye sure Da'?" Norman said without batting an eye."

"Norman, if she was forty years younger she'd be a dead

ringer for Robin Cook. Ye must've noticed, son, when ye kissed her, for instance – oh, Ah forgot, ye've never kissed her."

"Ah did wance, when Ah was drunk and had the courage up" Norman said.

"Well, did ye no' notice then?" Harry said.

"It was in the bathroom an' Ah just thought she was cleanin' her tooth at the time," Norman said.

"Whit made ye think that?" Harry asked, intrigued.

"She uses a *Brillo* pad," Norman said.

Harry felt his argument was pointless. Norman was obviously besotted by Bella – beard or no' beard. He looked over at Sadie, who was still lying on the floor and with Bella bending over her trying to bring her round. He thought of pouring a pan of cold water over Sadie but felt the shock would be too much for her. Not the shock of the water but the sight of a bending Bella. Harry said, turning to Norman, "It's the weans ye must think of, son. Wee weans love for to sit on their Mammy's knee an' stroke her hair, no' her beard. Faither's are allowed beards no' Mammy's."

Norman shook his head. "Ah think Ah'll throw masel' oot the windae," he said.

"That'll no' dae any good, Norman," Harry said, looking him in the eye.

"How no'?", Da'?",

"We're low doon son" Harry said.

Both turned at the sound of Sadie's groaning. She blinked her eys, rubbed them and sat up, still half asleep. "Whit – whit happened?" she mumbled.

"Ye took a wee turn, hen," Harry said, helping her to her feet.

Sadie turned and seeing Bella closed her eyes tightly and opened them again. But the vision was still there.

"Are ye a'right, Mammy?" Norman said, putting his arm around his mother's shoulder and giving her an affectionate squeeze.

"Aye, son," Sadie said, giving his hand a squeeze, "Ah'm composed noo"

Sadie stood up, fully erect, smoothed her apron down and cleared her throat "Ah've somethin' tae say," she began. "First of all Ah want tae apologise tae you, Bella, for faintin' like that.

Ah've never fainted in ma life before . . . well, just wance and that was wan Friday when Harry gave me his pey poke unopened. Another thing, Ah would like tae welcome Bella tae oor hoose. She is oor Norman's choice and Ah can see that she has made him very happy."

Norman kissed his mother's cheek. "Thanks, Mammy," he said.

"Turning to Balla, Sadie said, "Ah'd love for to have a chin-wag wi' ye Bella, but Ah'm frightened Ah'd come oot in a rash."

Bella laughed. "I'd like to visit the lady's room, Mrs McPhatter."

"In the close, go oot the door an' turn right and watch the puddle," Sadie said, opening the door.

Bella stepped out into the close and vanished right. Sadie turned to Norman, "Well, son, Ah'm just that pleased that you've found a lassie that tickles yer fancy."

"Not tae mention yer face," Harry piped up.

Sadie ignored her husband's facetious remark. "An as Ah said she's your choice and that's it. So, we'll jist enjoy oor night and if Bella wants tae put a bag ower her heid that's a'right tae."

"Aye, an' we'll cut a hole in it for her mooth," Harry added.

"That'll no' be necessary," Norman said. "Dae youse no' know whit day it is?"

"April Fool's Day?" Harry said.

"Naw," Norman said with a wry smile. "Ye know, there's a certain love song Ah think was just written for Bella this very day."

"An' whit's that, son?" Harry asked.

Before Norman could answer, Bella breezed in. She looked stunning – no beard and a pure white dazzling smile.

Sadie's jaw dropped and Harry spluttered.

"It *is* April Fools Day," Harry said.

"Naw, it's Saint Valentine's Day, intit?" Norman laughed.

"Ah just assumed Bella was the Bearded Lady in the circus," Sadie stammered.

"That was oor idea, Mammy," Norman chuckled, "Bella's no' the Bearded Lady in the circus. She's wan o' the clowns. A real joker, ma Bella!"

"Aye, well the joke's on us, right enough," Harry laughed,

"Noo, whit was that love song you said could have been written for Bella this day?"

"Aw, Da', can ye no' guess?" Norman said, slapping his father's back, "It's *My Funny Valentine*."

Everybody burst out laughing and Harry uncorked and poured out the Lanny.°

Two

░ ░ ░

HARRY AND SADIE FLELL BACK ON THE COUCH AND LAUGHED loudly as they recalled their first encounter with Norman's girl-friend.

"Aw, it was a scream right enough," Harry said. "Ah didnae think oor Norman had any humour in him."

"Oh, aye, he had. Sure he read the *Beano* right up till he was a good age – then he passed it ower tae you."

Harry nodded. "Ah, but Ah gave him ma *Dandy* in a swap."

Sadie sat pensive for a moment. "Ah wonder," she said, "whit happened tae Bella? Maybe her an' Norman got married. She might be wi' him in Canada!"

It was more a hope than a statement.

Harry screwed up his face, "She's probably become a politi-cian," he said.

"Whit makes ye say that?" Sadie asked, puzzled.

"They only take clowns in, don't they?" Harry replied with a wry smile. They laughed loudly.

"Mair tae the point," Harry added, "whit happened tae oor Norman?"

That was a situation that always nagged at Sadie. Although she had other problems flooding her mind, it was one thorn that would not be pulled out.

She stood up and took Harry's hand in hers. She squeezed it gently. "Ah always worry aboot Norman and Maggie," she said, "Thank God Ah've got you, Harry even though the dreams we had in oor young days wurnae all fulfilled."

"Like whit for instance?" Harry said, a little hurt.

"Well, like we always dreamt o' hivin' a nice wee bunglaow, a car, gran'weans runnin' roon oor feet, a' jumpin' and laughin' Sadie sighed deeply.

Harry suddenly felt that he had let Sadie down. He

34

remembered those dreams, those promises. But circumstances never permitted him to fullfil them.His wages in the factory merely allowed them to live day-to-day, week-to week, like most young couples – young dreamers. A bungalow was not for them and they were delighted when they received the keys of the house in Blotto Street. The name of the street didn't matter to them – although they signed the petition to have it changed. The point was that they *had* a house. Many young couples would have given their right arm to have a two-room-and-kitchen when they first got married. To most of them it was a case of staying with the in-laws – or a wee single-end – which was a lot better than living with the in-laws. The fact that in all cases the lavatory was on the stairhead where it served the three families on that stair landing, didn't matter. It was *Oor Hoose* and that's what mattered.

Harry sadly shook his head. "Aye, hen," he said, "Dreams – like a' young couples – maist o' them – faded just like the rest o' us."

Sadie squeezed his hand. "Ye have tae have them when ye're young, don't ye sweetheart?" she said sweetly.

Harry sighed. "Ah feel Ah've let ye doon, hen," he said.

Sadie shook her head. "Naw, naw, don't ever think that, Harry," she said softly. "We've had forty years together wi' oor ups an' downs an' Ah widnae chinge wan minute o' it."

Harry felt better and kissed her lightly on the cheek. "Thanks for that, hen" he said, "But look at us noo . . . here in *oor hoose* that they're gonny pull doon. No' much o' a legacy, is it?

"Ma legacy is you an' oor Norman an' Maggie," she said.

Harry smiled. "Y'know, hen," he said, "We've been in this hoose forty years and we've slagged it because o' the dampness an' a' the other faults we've found. We've had oor laughs an' tears an' Ah've called these wa's for everythin' at times. But Ah love it! It's *Oor Hoose – Oor Home.* We've had good neighbours, tae an' that's a big part o' happy livin'." Harry thought deeply for a moment. "They're a' away noo and there's a long silence up the buildin'. But there's wan consolation."

"Whit's that?" Sadie asked.

"Ah can go oot tae the lavvy withoot hivin' tae put on ma dressin'-gown," Harry said with a chuckle.

Sadie let out a yell. "*Dressin'-gown?*" she whooped, "When did you ever wear a dressin'-gown? It took me a' ma time tae stoap ye goin' oot that door in yer long johns."

Sadie dug him in the ribs with her elbow and Harry laughed loudly.

"Here," he said, rubbing his hands together, "let's have a wee dram, Ah mean it *is* oor anniversary."

Harry went over to the table and poured out two large glassfuls. "Here," he said, handing a glass to Sadie, "Hiv some Buckfast."

"Aw, naw, no' Buckfast," Sadie said, pushing the glass away, "Know somethin'," she added, "*You* take oan the persona of whitever ye're drinkin'. "

Harry spluttered. "Whit dae ye mean?" he asked, drawing his eyebrows together.

Sadie drew herself up to her full height. "Harry", she said, "if you drink that Buckfast ye'll suddenly think you're Friar Tuck and go aboot the hoose beltin' oot the Gregorian Chant. That's a'right for Buckfast Abbey, Harry, but no' for the hoose."

"Ye're talkin' rubbish," Harry sniped.

"Am Ah?" Sadie replied. "Whit aboot the night ye drank a boattle o' sherry?"

"Whit aboot it?" Harry said.

"Ye went aboot thinkin' ye were Julio Iglesius," Sadie said, referring to the Spanish pop idol.

"Ach, rubbish!" Harry replied. screwing up his nose.

"Rubbish, is it?" Sadie sniped, "Wan gless o' Johnny Walker and we get the Hielin' Fling a' night. and whit aboot the night ye downed hauf-a-pint o' gin an' orange – wi' a pony chaser?"

"So what?" Harry said, trying to disinterest.

"So whit?" Sadie repeated. "Next day ye were oot leadin' the Orange Walk – oan a *hoarse*." Sadie threw up her arms.

"So, whit's wrang wi' that?" Harry said.

"We're Catholics, Harry," Sadie said, exasperated.

Harry shrugged his shoulders. "Well, Ah love music," he said timidly and in way of mitigation.

But Sadie's thoughts were now elsewhere.

"Y'know, Harry," she said at last, "Oor Norman loved music,

tae. Remember how he used tae sing as loud as he could, when he went oot tae the lavvy?"

"Only when he sat doon oan a cauld pan," Harry said facetiously.

"Norman had a great voice," Sadie said in her son's defence. "Ah always thought he might consider a showbusiness career, Ah keep watchin' the telly, thinkin' that wan day he'll suddenly appear on the screen."

"Aye, ye're fond o' they David Attenborough programmes, right enough," Harry said, referring to that expert's wild animal behavioural programmes and ducking down in case Sadie took a swipe at him.

But Sadie's mind was far away. "Aw, don't talk aboot oor Norman," she said, dabbing the corner of her eye.

"Ah try no' tae," Harry said, "but he keps creepin' up. Ah'll never forget that day ye brought him hame frae Rottenrow, a' covered an' snug in a wee tartan shawl."

Sadie smiled at the thought.

"Aye, jist a week auld, he was," she said. "Ah brought him in in ma airms an' you tipped-toed ower an' moved the shawl back an' stared doon at the wee soul – remember?"

"Oh, aye," Harry sighed, "Ah remember fine. Ah stared, an' stared, an' stared."

"Did ye think Ah'd brought hame the wrang wean?" Sadie asked.

"Ah thought ye'd brought hame the afterbirth," Harry said with a straight face.

Sadie gave him a playful push.

"That's nae wey tae talk aboot yer son," she scolded.

"Just kiddin', hen," Harry said. "that was a loat o' years ago."

"Aye," Sadie said, with a faraway look, "a loat o' years. We'd been merried for just eighteen months when Norman arrived. Remember oor weddin' night?"

Harry nodded. "Of course, Ah dae," he said, "you were greetin'."

"So were you," Sadie said.

"Ah'd just cerried you ower the threshold and intae this hoose," Harry said with a slight grunt.

."Aye, an' Ah've had tae cairry you ower it many a time since.

Harry laughed.

"Well, Ah'm gled ye remember oor weddin' night, Harry," she said, "We had oor first argument," that night.

"Ah don't remember *that*," Harry said drawing his brows.

"Oh, aye," Sadie said. "Mind? You wanted tae go straight tae bed an' Ah wanted tae go tae a pantomime in the *Pavilion* and have a good laugh."

"An' who won?" Harry asked curiously.

"We baith did," Sadie said.

"Ye saw a pantomime n' had a good laugh, then?" Harry asked.

"Ah did," Sadie said,

"At the *Pavilion?*" Harry asked.

"In bed," Sadie laughed.

Harry smiled. "Aye, Ah remember noo," he said "Ye lay a' night eatin' a boax o' Cowans chocolates. When Ah kissed ye it was like *Willie Wonka's Chocolate Factory*."

"Ah was addicted tae them," Sadie said, smacking her lips, "Ah could've ate Cowans sweeties tae a baun' playin'."

"Ye did," Harry said, "Ye had the wireless on an' Geraldo's baun' was on a' night.

"Ye had Mad Cowans disease,that's for sure," Harry said.

"Want another drink?" Sadie said, rising and going to the table.

"Well, if you insist," Harry said nonchalantly.

Sadie poured and handed him the glass.

"Here", she said "get that doon ye . . . and nae funny business,"

"Whit dae ye mean, 'nae funny business'? Whit is this drink?" he said, knitting his brows.

"It's *Jack Daniels*," Sadie said.

"Ye know Ah'll no' touch any drink that's called efter a person. Ah'm superstitious that wey."

"Ye drink Johnny Walker, don't ye?" Sadie retorted.

"Ah, but he's wan o' us, a true Scotsman." Harry said.

"Harry, you would drink the contents oot o' a coo's bladder," Sadie said.

"Only if it was a Highland coo," Harry replied with a chuckle.

"Besides," he went on "whit de ye mean, 'nae funny business'?"

Sadie puckered her lip. "Well", she said, "that *Jack Daniels* is Kentucky bourbon. An' knowin' how drink affects you, Ah do nut want you tae be struttin' aboot the hoose like Clint Eastwood."

"That's cowboy booze, so it is. Y'know, in the pitctures they call that Redeye." said Harry

"They called you that doon at the broo," Sadie said with a wry smile.

Harry was glad that Sadie still had her sense of humour despite the worry hanging over her head. "Ah wonder where their next oaffer of a hoose will be?" he found himself saying.

"It'll need tae be somethin' better than they've oaffered us so far," Sadie said sternly.

Harry nodded. "Ye're right, Sadie," he agreed, "These high flats should be torn doon. Ah mean, look at that last wan they oaffered us on the fifteenth flair. Whit a con, that was. It's a great view they said. Whit rubbish! Ah stepped on tae the verandah tae see for masel' and Ah was nut impressed wan bit."

"Nae view?" Sadie said.

"Nae verandah," Harry groaned.

"Ah jist don't want tae leave here, Harry. ma whole life's been here," Sadie said with emotion. "We brought up oor weans here. It's a wee hoose full o' love and memories. Ah hate tae leave it. It jist breaks ma heart tae think aboot it."

Harry saw how upset Sadie was and tried to bring her down to earth by pointing out the warts.

"It was a wee bit damp, right enough," he said.

"So, whit's a bit o' dampness here an' there?" Sadie said in defence of her home.

"Well, you complained plenty aboot it," Harry argued.

"Ye've got tae complain tae these factors noo an' then tae keep them on their toes for mair serious things," Sadie said.

"Aye, well, maybe ye're right right, hen," Harry said and put his arms around her shoulder.

"Ah keep thinkin' o' the weans growin' up," Sadie said.

Harry smiled as he too thought of the weans. Maggie would be about ninety-two now, he reckoned. Not in years but in ugly appearance. He remembered how cats used to hunch their backs and spit everytime she passsed. Of how she walked into a dairy one day and all the milk turned sour.

But, like Sadie, he loved her – despite her cone shaped head. She was the mould for all dunces caps in the school. Norman had a similar affect on all who came into contact with him. He once went with the school on a cultural trip to Paris and was chucked out of the Louvre when, after gazing at the *Mona Lisa*, it took on the appearance of a toothless man. Of how fame was once within Norman's grasp when he was invited to be Cheta's understudy in a Tarzan film.

"Ah was jist thinkin' o' Maggie and Norman masel' there," Harry said.

"It's hard tae forget them," Sadie said sadly.

Harry nodded. "Ah know, Ah've tried oaften enough," he said.

Suddenly there was a loud rap on the door. Harry and Sadie's eyes met.

"Who could that be?" Sadie said."Naebody's been up this close for ages."

Harry shrugged. "Probably somebody wantin' directions," he said.

Sadie hurried to answer the door. Minnie Magee stood on the doorstep. Small and slim she wore an alopeciac fox-fur around her scraggy neck. She smiled broadly.

"Hello, Mrs McPhatter" she said.

"Come in, come in Mrs Magee," Sadie beamed She was pleased to see her old neighbour. Minnie Magee had brought a little bit class to the close, Sadie had always thought. She remembered the foxfur when it was a cub and how Minnie, who once lived on the second landing before being one the first tenants to be re-located, kept herself to herself except when she was gossiping about other people. Minnie Magee spoke with "jorries in her mooth". She had obviously taken elocution lessons in her younger days and her *panloaf* accent was admired by everyone up number twenty-seven except for those who were so engrossed in the Glasgow dialect that they couldn't understand a word she said. Sadie steered Minnie to the couch and saw her comfortably seated.

"I'm sorry to impose on you like this, Mrs McPhatter," Minnie said, removing her foxfur and placing at her side, patting it on the head.

"Aw, don't be daft, Mrs Magee," Sadie said.

"Ah can see ye're a bit distressed, Mrs Magee," Harry volunteered "Is it yer teeth?"

Minnie's hand came up to her mouth. "What's wrong with my teeth?" she asked worriedly.

"Ye've got them in upside doon," Harry said.

Sadie butted in immediately to avoid Minnie any embarrassment. "Er . . . would you like a wee cup of tea, Mrs Magee?" she went on.

"Oh, that would be lovely, Mrs McPhatter," Minnie smiled and leaned back on the couch."

"Or maybe you would like something a wee bit stronger," Sadie said as an afterthought. "Harry and me are celebratin' oor Ruby Weddin'."

Minnie Magee clapped hae hands together. "Oh, that's lovely!" she said. "I don't usually drink alcohol but seeing this is a special occasion . . ."

"Right!" Sadie interrupted, "Harry – a sherry for Mrs Magee."

"A *whisky*," Minnie said quickly.

"Er . . . right . . . Harry, pour Mrs Magee a wee whisky," Sadie said a little surprised.

"A *double*," Minnie said quickly. Sadie's eyes widened and Harry poured out a glassful of single malt.

Handing it to Minnie's eager and outstretched hand , he said. "Right, get that doon yer thrapple."

Minnie Magee knocked back the single malt in a single gulp. She smacked her lips and handed the empty glass back to Harry with an obvious request for a repeat in her glinting eye. Harry poured another which vanished down Minnie's throat as fast as the first. He took the glass from her without looking at her face as he could see his precious bottle of *Glenmorange* disappearing much too quickly.

"Here's wishing you another forty years of happiness," Minnie said, "nodding towards the table while catching Sadie's eye.

"Oh, you've finished your drink," Sadie said, taking the hint. "Harry," she said, nodding towards the table.

Harry capitulated and handing Minnie her empty glass half filled it only to have his arm grabbed and brought down to tip the bottle over and fill the glass to the brim.

Minnie demolished the drink, after toasting Sadie and Harry, wiped her mouth with the back of her hand and cleared her throat.

"Er . . . have you had an encounter with Mr Hector McNab yet, Mrs McPhatter?" Minnie asked.

Sadie nodded. "I have," she said.

Minnie Magee stuck her nose in the air and sniffed loudly. "He's a terrible man," she said with a touch of venom. "Do you know," she went on, her voice falling to a whisper, "That man made a pass at me – one of a sexual nature!" Minnie shuffled in her chair.

Sadie and Harry's eyes met and Sadie detected a fleeting smile crossing her husband's face. Harry cleared his throat, "Er . . . was he drunk at the time?" he said.

She shook her head, missing the sarcasim behind the question.

"Whit did he dae Mrs Magee?" Sadie asked.

"He . . . er . . . touched my knee," Minnie said, her voice shaking.

"Ur ye sure he wisnae drunk?" Harry repeated. For although he had no time for Hector McNab he could never in a million years see him making a pass at Minnie Magee . . . Big Jessie Campbell up the stairs, *yes*, Minnie Magee, *no*!

Minnie shook her head. "I'm sure he was not drunk" she said, "although I could smell peppermint coming from his breath when I gave him mouth-to-mouth resucitation," she said.

"Oh, did he have a heart attack?" Sadie asked in disbelief.

"He said he hadn't and was lying on the floor looking for a pound coin he had dropped. But I think that that was just an excuse to look up my skirt." Minnie was adamant.

"He must've been drunk," Harry said, keeping a straight face.

"Ah could never have believed that o' him," Sadie volunteered.

"Well, I'm not surprised," Minnie said, pride in her voice." I *do* have that effect on some men. Some men just lose control of their emotions when they are in my presence. The late Mr Magee used to get very jealous when he saw the attention men gave me when I entered a room."

Harry gulped. "Ah'd better go an' put ma strait jaicket on before Ah go berserk," he said facetiously, pouring himself a stiff dram. Minnie coughed loudly her hand outstretched. The message was not lost on Harry who filled the glass which Minnie downed in a single gulp.

"Er . . . did ye come doon for to see us for anythin' special Mrs Magee?" Sadie asked curiously.

Minnie shook her head. "No, no," she said, " I just felt I had to come back to the old place again. The late Mr Magee and I spent many happy years up this close. We raised our children here." Minnie dabbed the corner of her eye with her handkerchief, the drink taking effect.

Sadie understood how her old neighbour felt. "We were a' shocked when Mr Magee passed away," she said.

"Oh, yes, poor Horace" Minnie said, dabbing her eyes once more.

"*Horace*" Harry yelled.

"His dear mother was a fan of *Hungry Horace* and called him after him," Minnie said. "His father was delighted that Horace was an only child because his wife was also a great fan of *The Broons.*"

Harry could understand that.

"How did . . . er . . . Horace die, Mrs Magee?" Sadie asked, showing interest.

"Oh, I remember that day vividly," Minnie said. "I had mislaid my spectacles and Horace had been begging me to syringe his ear."

"He had wax in them?" Sadie inquired.

"Enough to make six L.P.'s." Minnie said. "Anyway, I fumbled in the drawer looking for the syringe. All the while Mr Magee was standing singing an operatic aria."

"Pavarotti?" Harry piped up

"Oh yes, he *was* rotten," Minnie replied. "But he was not really singing an aria. It was the pain in his ears that was making him scream out loud. Anyway my groping hand found the syringe and I stuck it into his ear and stopped his suffering."

43

"Did you blow the wax out?" Sadie innocently asked

"I blew his brains out," Minnie said in a flat tone. "With not having my glasses on I had picked up his old army revolver by mistake."

"Ah never knew that," Harry said.

"That I had mistakenly killed poor Horace?" Minnie asked.

"Naw, that he was ever in the army." Harry said.

"Oh, yes, Minnie said with pride. "He served with the great Gunga Din."

"The famous water boy" Harry commented.

"The *what* boy?" Minnie asked.

"Water," Harry repeated.

"No thanks. I'll just have my whisky straight," Minnie said, holding up her glass.

Harry's eyes looked to heaven and he shook his head and refilled Minnie's glass – the contents disappearing in a gulp, followed by a smacking of lips.

"The detective who came up was very understanding," Minnie went on.

"He believed yer story?" Sadie asked in disbelief.

"Oh, yes," Minnie replied with a knowing smile." He found me, stunningly attractive he could hardly keep his hands off me . . . especially my knees."

"Yer knees seem to be irrisistable," Harry said facetiously

"I *do* have that effect on men," Minnie said. removing her top teeth, polishing them on her sleeve before replacing them. She smiled broadly. "Horace, bless him, used to go into a frenzy when we were at the beach and I would roll up my trousers past my knees so that I could go into the water for a paddle."

"Maybe he thought ye should use the toilets like everybody else," Harry said flatly.

"To go into the water for a paddle?" Minnie said in surprise.

"Oh, Ah thought ye said a *piddle*," Harry replied with a straight face.

"Ah must say you're lookin' well, Mrs Magee," Sadie said quickly.

"Call me Minnie, Mrs McPhatter," Minnie said. "After all we've lived up the same close for most of our married lives."

"Aye, true," Sadie said. "And you can call me Sadie."

"Oh, yesh, it's jusht wonderful to shee the old place again, Shadie. Thish place of sho many happy memories." Minnie sighed deeply, her inebriation showing through.

"Aye, yer full o' nostalgia Minnie, that it?" Harry said.

"Only on my knees, Mr McPhatter. Horace used to rub them every night with *Deep Heat* but would go into a frenzy before he could finish and I had to climb into bed just half rubbed."

"Ah've gone into bed hauf cut many a time," Harry admitted.

"I really came round to shay how much I admired your shtand by not allowin' that wee turd McNab shunt yoush into any place yoush don't want to go to. Keep shticking to your gunsh Shadie."

Sadie puffed out her chest. "Ye don't like yer high-rise flat then Minnie?"

Minnie grimaced. "I hate it, Shadie," she moaned. "Twenty-seven shtoreys high and lifts that never work. It's jusht terrible everytime the lifts go off. When that happens I jusht shtorm down to McNab's offish and give him a piece of my mind." Minnie Magee's mettle was up.

"How many up are you, Minnie," Sadie inquired.

"I'm on the ground floor," Minnie replied.

"In that case ye don't need tae worry aboot the lifts, then," Harry said.

"Ah, but thatsh shelfish," Minnie scolded. "Do ash the *Good Book* shaid *love your neighbour*." Minnie's hand went to heart and she looked towards heaven.

"That's a helluva loat o' lovin when ye're steyin' up a multi-storey block," Harry said.

"It's the people above me that I feel sorry for," Minnie went on, especially the animals."

"Ye're an animal lover then?" Sadie said.

"I am." Minnie said. " got it from Horace."

"He was an animal lover?" Harry asked.

"No, he looked like a giraffe," Minnie said. "Always a very proud expression on his face if you know what I mean?"

"And ye think the animials up your buildin' get a raw deal, then, Minnie?" Sadie said, knitting her brows.

"As well as raw pawsh, Shadie," Minnie said, adding, "Do you know there's a young woman on the twenty-seventh floor who has a lovely rottweiler called snowflake – a lovely, friendly dog was snowflake. It would never pass by me without wagging its tail and I would bend down and pat it it." Minnie sighed. "But," she went on, shaking her head sadly, "the poor dog got depressed having to climb those stairs every day because the lift were always off and I was shocked when I met that lady and her dog the other day."

"Why was that, Mrs Magee?" Harry asked curiously.

"That beautiful rottweiler was now a dachshund," Minnie Magee dabbed her left eye.

"Nae wonder the dug was peeved," Sadie said, shaking her head.

"Yes, and not only that," Minnie went on, "that good natured wee dog had lost its happy disposition."

"How dae ye know, Minnie?" Sadie asked.

"Well," Minnie said,"Just the other day I bent down to pat it, just as I always do and know what it did?"

"Whit?" Harry said, knitting his eyebrows,

"It . . . it bit me," Minnie said, shaking her head.

"Oh, that can be dangerous," Sadie blurted. "Did ye get a tetanus jag?"

Minnie Magee shook her head. "No, I did not," she said. "I knew the wee darling didn't mean it. It was right out of character. I didn't want to get the wee soul into trouble."

"Whit *did* ye do?" Sadie asked.

"I kicked it as hard as I could," Minnie said, dabbing her right eye.

"Ye kicked it?" Sadie said surprised.

"I did," Minnie said, "Right on the balls."

Sadie gasped at Minnie's uncharacteristic statement. Harry's whisky must be taking its toll, she reckoned. "Good for you, Minnie," Sadie heard herself saying.

"Yep," Minnie said, "I would've bit it back but my teeth were at the cleaners."

"Aye, well Harry and me will never accept a hoose we don't want," Sadie said.

"Good!" Minnie exclaimed."Don't you let that auld swine McNab shuffle you into wan o' the towerin' infernals," she said.

"Too true," Sadie agreed.

"Ma . . . er . . . my Horace complains about that hoose every night when he comes tae me."

"But Horace is *deid*," Harry snapped. "He's up there wi' Gunga Din in that great water hole in the sky."

"But he still comes to see me . . . every night," Minnie insisted.

"Tae rub yer knees?" Harry said facetiously.

"Harry!" Sadie scolded her husband for being insensitive. Harry shrugged.

"When I stretch out my hand it goes right through him," Minnie said, ignoring Harry's sarcasm.

"Sadie does that wi' me," Harry said with a wry smile.

Minnie's eyebrows rose. "Her hand goes right through you?" she said with surprise.

"Her haun goes right through ma poackets," Harry grinned.

"Someday I hope to join him in his celeshtial home," Minnie said with delight, "Where there are no lifts to worry about and everything is heavenly."

"Where the dugs are gumsy as well, eh?" Harry piped up.

"Horace says there's a Celtic and Rangers team up there and they take turns at winning. One week Celtic win and the next week Rangers win. Everybody is happy and the Rangers fans wear green and white and the Celtic fans wear blue and white."

"Are you sure it's heaven Horace is in?" Harry grumped.

Minnie nodded. "Oh, yes," she said, "Horace is a keen football fan. Sometimes he appears to me wearing his colours – magenta and purple."

"Whit team's *that*?" Harry asked.

"That's not a team," Minnie said. "That's the colours of his face after I blew his brains out."

"Did Horace . . . er . . . never complain tae ye aboot that?" Sadie asked.

"Oh, no, in fact he thanked me," Minnie said.

"Thanked ye?" Harry and Sadie said in unison.

"Yes, he said he could hear perfectly for the first time and told me to drop *Earwax* a line congratulating them on their new powerful drops."

Harry and Sadie glanced knowingly at each other.

Sadie cleared her throat. "Well, Minnie," she began, "Ah

really appreciate ye coming tae visit us. It gets very lonely livin' up the close oorsel's."

"I know, Shadie," Minnie said. "I missh the old place too, although I do admit I used hate going down to the midden in the dark. "

"How did ye no' go doon durin' the day, then?" Sadie said.

"Oh I didn't want everyone to see my garbage," Minnie said, screwing up her face."People are nosey, you know. I always carefully watched what I was throwing out."

"Ah'm sure you had nothin' tae hide, Minnie," Sadie smiled.

Minnie blushed. "Well . . . er . . . there were the empty bottles," she said, averting her eyes.

"Horace liked a nip?" Harry said in disbelief.

"Oh yes." Minnie said, "On his back, on his chest he didn't care where."

"He liked a nip oan his back – his chist – ?" Harry was dumbfounded. "Horace Magee, the quiet man of number twenty-seven."

"*Nip*?" Minnie cried, "No, no – I thought you said *whip*. Horace loved his whip. Every Saturday night I would ladle into him. He always said Saturday night was a night for enjoyment." Minnie smiled as she recalled those Saturday nights.

"Ah don't believe it," Sadie said, "He was such a gentleman . Ah canny imagine him enjoyin' you whippin' him."

"Believe me," Minnie said, "Horace was never mair happier than when I was giving him a tanking."

Sadie glanced at Harry who shrugged and said, "It takes all sorts. Ah did notice that ye put yer classical music records on helluva loud on a Setturday. right enough."

"I did." Minnie said, "Most people thought it was due to Horace's ear wax but it was really to muffle his cries of pain, Horace loved pain. 'It was the makings of a man,' he always said."

"Aye, well, he must've been happy when you blew his heid aff," Harry said cynically.

"Ye was never charged wi' that, Minnie?" Sadie asked, puzzled.

"No, never," Minnie said. "The investigating officer fell in love with me and put Horace's demise down to a fatal accident done when he was poking about his ear with the barrel of his gun."

Harry nodded. "Well, Ah suppose it was the ultimate torture for Horace. Ah don't think he would've wanted tae go any other wey – except maybe by thumbscrew or somethin'."

Minnie shook her head. "No, he didn't like the thumbscrew I had to swap it for a pair of clappers. Oh, how Horace loved them!" Minnie clapped her hands gleefully together.

"Well, Minnie," Sadie went on, " Ah really canny thank ye enough for comin' roon and Ah'm sorry ye don't like the high-flats."

"I hate them, Shadie", Minnie said, " and don't you let that wee bachle McNab talk you into accepting one. You know, I'm sure the height affected my poor Horace's health."

"No' as much as that gun did," Harry quipped. Minnie ignored the sarcasm.

"It undoubtedly affected his ears," Minnie added.

"But ye steyed on the ground floor," Sadie reminded her.

"He had a low pulse rate," Minnie said in way of mitigation. "Except when I was giving him a hiding," she added.

"Ah widnae think livin' on the ground floor would've affected his ears, Minnie."

"Ah but Horace spent a lot of time up on the twenty-seventh floor, Shadie," Minnie said. "Being a dog lover, he spent lots of time with that dachshund that used to be a rottweiler. He felt sorry for it and its mistress. He was kind that way, my Horace." Minnie spoke with pride.

"Was Horace interested in foreign dugs, then?" Harry asked puzzled.

"What do you mean?" Minnie replied suspiciously.

"Well, Ah mean – dachshund, rottweiler – German dugs."

"No, no," Minnie said, "Horace was interested in all dogs. He particularly took a fancy to a little Chinese dog he saw in a pet shop. But when he heard the price of it . . . "

"Shihtzu," Harry volunteered.

"I think he did," Minnie said.

"Ye said he spent a lot o' time on the twenty-seventh floor wi' that daschund?"

"Oh, yes. I didn't mind that," Minnie said, "but he *did* arrive home smelling strongly of Chanel Number Five. He said that the big-bosomed blonde girl who owned the dog sprayed it on the poor pooch to hide the doggy odours."

Minnie rose to leave. She staggered slightly and Sadie rushed to steady her. She steered Minnie towards the door.

"Now, don't you forget, Shadie," Minnie said, turning. "Do not let that wee fat pig McNab talk you into anything for *we arra people.*" Minnie threw her arms in the air and staggered into the closemouth singing with gusto – *We Are the Champions of the World.*

Harry turned to Sadie. "Well, that was a turn up for the book, eh?"

Sadie grinned. "Poor auld sowel," she said, "That's a' baloney. Her man didnae die wi' a bullet in the heid. He had a heart attack."

"Nae wonder," Harry said, "A' that visitin' the twenty-seventh flair – wi' a dug at the end o' it attached tae a big blonde."

Sadie laughed. "Ye can bet a' Horace was interested in *was* the dug. He was a nice wee man. Ah think the shock o' his passin' has affected poor Minnie's mind."

Harry shook his head sadly. "Aw, she's definitely away wi' the fairies, that's for sure," he said. Then, smacking his lips, he added. "Made me right thirsty," he said, looking at Sadie.

"Ah thought it might," Sadie said with a twinkle in her eye.

"Ah . . . er . . . think Ah'll just pop doon tae the pub for a pint," Harry said, almost apologetically.

"Aye, away ye go. Ah'll tidy up," Sadie said.

Harry kissed Sadie lightly on the cheek and stepped into the close.

The pub was just a few hundred yards away and Harry turned up his coat collar almost covering his mouth. There was a sting in the cold air and he shivered a little. Going to the pub wasn't the same these days Harry had decided. The pub itself had become all plastic. There was the ubiqutious karaoke and gone were the days when he could stand at the bar sipping his pint and chatting to Erchie the barman. Now you needed to be armed with a megaphone to be heard and some of the singers, who thought they were Elvis, were merely an anagram of that famous name – Vile – plural. He missed the dust of the street, the lighted windows of the tenements – dotted yellowsquares all the way down the street. Dirty chimneys billowing out smoke. The odd barney belting out from half-open windows. His was the only grey tenement left standing – a fortress against the might of Fuehrer McNab. The corner boys had gone. There used to be six or seven of them hanging about the corner of the street just watching the world go by. Most of them on the dole despite this world of television and personal computers. Harry still enjoyed a pint or two and was glad that Erchie, karaoke or no', still hadn't done away with the domino box. The *Come Inn* pub he knew of old had been demolished along with the dusty tenement buildings but, thankfully, had been rebuilt by the astute brewery owners.

Harry had been a patron of the *Come Inn* long before he met Sadie that night in *Barrowland Ballroom*, in the Gallowgate. In his younger days he was the dapper, brylcreemed man about town. Youth would be a better word. But there was no doubt about it, Harry was the envy of his pals. If anybody could get the girl it would be Harry. And. although he was in the autumn of his years, he was still a fine-looking man and felt fortunate that he could still use the Brylcreem.

The pub was quiet when Harry pushed his way through the heavy door with its gleaming brass handles. He stood inside the doorway feeling the welcoming warmth of the central heating system. His eyes scanned the room. Erchie was behind the bar polishing glasses and the only customers were two young women sitting, sipping some orange concoction at a table. Harry was glad there was no blasting karaoke in progress. Erchie spotted him.

"Harry, auld son," he bellowed in greeting, adding, "Usual?"

Harry nodded and sauntered up to the bar where Erchie was pouring the final topping on his pint of export. Harry sipped the cold beer, wiping the froth from his mouth with the back of his hand.

"Quiet the night, Erchie!" Harry exclaimed.

Erchie shrugged. "Aye, it gies the auld eardrums a chance tae recuperate."

"Don't mention ears," Harry said, with a mock grimace.

"How's it gaun, then?" Erchie said. "Ah heard you an' Sadie

51

were hivin' a wee bit bother wi' auld McNab. Youse are the last wans up the close, eh?"

Harry nodded. "We hivnae been oaffered anythin' that suits us and ye know Sadie, dead fussy."

"Well, she could nae have been that fussy when she married you, Harry," Erchie said, a twinkle in his eye.

"Here, whit's the gemme?" Harry sniped, hurt.

"Just kiddin', Harry, just kiddin'," Erchie laughed, slapping Harry's arm.

"Aye, well, we've been married forty years," Harry said, "This is oor anniversary – this very day – forty years, eh!" Harry stuck out his chest.

"Aye, well, she's a sticker, Sadie is," Erchie said, clicking his tongue. "Especially knowin' how flighty you were in yer younger days. Ye wurnae hauf a man for the ladies, eh?" Erchie gave Harry a knowing wink.

Harry nodded and grinned. "Och, aye," he said, " but it was nothin' ever serious."

"Well, it disnae matter noo," Erchie went on, "ye're well past it."

Harry eyes furrowed. "Whit dae ye mean, *well past it*?" he snapped.

"Ye're an auld man noo, Harry," Erchie turned the screw.

"Ah might be a bit aulder," Harry said, "but Ah've still got the same equipment Ah had the day Ah got married. Right enough, Ah suppose, there's a few extras in ma life – high blood pressure pills, ma asthma nebuliser, rheumatism pills an' that, now."

Erchie hid his grin. "So, ye still think ye could attract the opposite sex, then, eh?"

"Are you suggestin' Ah couldnae get a young beautful wumman tae get interested in me?" Harry said with a hurt expression.

"Ah'm suggestin' that no' only could ye no' get a young beautiful wumman tae look at ye, ye couldnae even get an ugly *auld* wumman tae look at ye. And, goin' further, ye couldnae get an ugly auld *man* tae look at ye." Erchie was stirring Harry's emotions and enjoying it.

"Is that so?" Harry said. "We'll see." Turning to the two girls sitting sipping their concoction, he nodded towards them.

"Who are they?" he said.

"Them?" Erchie shrugged and added," They're French . . ."

Harry stopped him with his hand up. "Say no more," he said. "French is ma second language," Ah'll show ye that Ah hivnae lost the auld charm. Ye're gonny eat yer words . . . watch this."

"But . . ." Erchie started.

"Nae buts," Harry said. "Jist watch and learn."

Erchie shrugged. Who was he to doubt the great Don Juan? He grinned as Harry sauntered nonchalantly over to the girls.

"Vooly voos madam masels," he said. "Welcome tae Glesca the city of arch-i-tekture. City of the greatest arch-it-ekt in the world – Rennie McIntosh. Not only did Auld Rennie design buildin's an' that, his surname should gie youse a clue. McIntosh, he invented toaffees and raincoats. and if ye got indigestion his first name should gie youse another clue – Rennie. Take two an' yer wind vanishes." Harry was in full stride. "Glesca," he went on, "Is latin for *The Dear Green Place* – except if you're a Rangers supporter and then it's *The Dear Blue Place.*"

Erchie watched all this with interest and the girls glanced at each other and giggled.

One of the girls smiled broadly and said, "Enchante!"

Harry furrowed his brows and looked quizically over at Erchie. "Is yer ladies' toilet oot o' action?" he shouted.

Erchie shook his head. "Naw, whit are ye askin' that for?"

Harry gestured with his thumb to the girls, "They are askin' for a chanty," he said.

"Away ye go," Erchie said, laughing and dismissing Harry with a wave of his hand. "Enchante means *enchanted.*"

"Oh!" Harry said, just a little embarrassed. Turning to the girls, he said. "Ah beg yer pardon, hen or should Ah say, 'I beg your pardon, *poulet!*" Using his poshest voice he continued. "It's French for hen, youse know. Youse'll think it's a French word but it's no'. Poulet is a Glesca word. We hiv been usin' it for years – it is a contraption we hing up in oor kitchens and hing the washin' oan."

The girls were open-eyed and sat giggling.

"Would youse like a packet of crisps for tae eat wi' yer booze?" Harry asked dipping his hand into his pocket. "Sorry, but we don't have hoarse flavour. Ah believe that youse are partial tae a bit of hoarse where youse come frae. We do nut eat oor hoarses here, although some o' them Ah've backed should've been chewed up an' spat oot."

The girls sat listening to every word. Harry strode on. He was pleased with himself. Of how he had captured the girls' interest.

Yes, he thought, the old charm was still working. "Another thing," he went on, "Opera, youse Franch are daft on the Opera. Ah have heard of that marvellous French Opera House the – *Milan LaScala* – "

Erchie, listening intently, shook his head despairingly. Harry went on. "Ah know a' aboot that wonderful wee singer youse hiv . . . er . . . her that's known as the . . . er . . .the . . . pigeon."

"Sparra, Harry," Erchie corrected.

"Aye, the Sparra," Harry repeated. "Her real name was . . . er . . . was . . ." Harry looked pleadingly at Erchie."

"Piaff," Erchie said.

"Aw ye don't have tae be like that," Harry said, "Ah only asked ye a question.

"That her name, " Erchie said, "*Piaff – Edith Piaff.*"

"Aw, Ah misunderatood," Harry said. "Well, girls," he said, turning to the giggling duo, "Let me shows youse a bit of Glasgow hospitality.Would youse like a rerr terr? How aboot a wee hauf, eh?"

"Away ye go, ya dirty auld swine," the girls echoed as they rose to make for the exit. "Come on, Felicity," the smaller girl said, pushing her friend towards the door, "let this auld man get on his zimmer and collect his pension."

The girls stormed out and left Harry with his mouth wide open. Harry turned to Erchie who was shaking with laughter.

"You telt me they were French," Harry snapped at the barman.

"Ye didnae let me finish," Erchie said, "They're *French Poalishers*! They work in the coaffin factory roon' the coarner."

"Ah thought they had a dead pan look aboot them," Harry said.

"Aye, well, it's yer anniversary an' Ah think ye should be gettin' up the road and get a tightner in ye."

"Aye, ye're right," Harry agreed, "Sadie will probably be gettin' ma tea ready. We love Italian food, we love eatin' spaghetti."

"Bolognaise?" Erchie asked.

Harry shook his head. "Naw, we keep oor claes on," he said.

"Er . . . aye . . . that's no' whit Ah meant," Erchie said, "but it disnae matter. Youse – er – like Italian food, eh?"

"Oh, aye, "Harry said, "if we canny get spaghetti there's nothin' for tae beat that other great Italian dish."

"Whit's that?" Erchie asked.

"A fish supper," Harry said.

Erchie laughed.

"Ye've put me in the notion," Harry said, his mouth watering at the thought. "Ah think Ah'll pop intae Mario' on the wey hame an get a couple o' fish suppers, wi' two pickles."

"Right, away ye go," Erchie said, "Ye're puttin' *me* in the notion."

Harry laughed and headed for the door. Turning, he called, "Goognight the noo, Erchie – and, as they say in French – *Arividerci.*"

Erchie gave him a dismissive wave and Harry was gone.

* * *

Sadie wondered what what keeping Harry. She busied herself tidying up. Finished, she stood in the middle of the floor an surveyed the room. She listened to the quietness outside. She tought she could hear the shrill voice of wee Alice Campbell hurrying up the stairs after leaving the *Arcadia Cinema*, in London Road, which was showing a Frankenstein picture.

"*O-open . . . pee-en,*" wee Alice would scream, terrified as she dashed up the stairs two at a time. Then the thump, thump, thumping at her door. The noise of the girls playing shops in the close or Peever outside her window.

She thought of Old Jake McGroarty who, every Saturday night, sat outside on the stairs and bellowed out *Nellie Dean* at the top of his drunken voice. It was a weekly ritual for Old Jake and no Saturday night would have been complete without the sound of *Nellie Dean* echoing up the stairs. It was a signal for Jake's frustrated wife, Helen, to come down the stairs and steer her husband safely up to his waiting bed. All had gone now and while some of the tenants had gone to the high-rise flats others were luckier and had landed four-in-the block or terraced houses with the greenery of the back gardens and the openess of it all. The city had ceased building the 'multi-storeys' although some tenants enjoyed them. The luxury of an inside bathroom and toilet was the appetiser.

Sadie wondered when the axe would fall and she and Harry would be forced to move? For that moment would surely come and not only would she be leaving the house she occupied for forty years but would be leaving all its memories – of the dreadful wallpaper Harry walked in with not long after they were married. Bright green with huge, yellow sunflowers. It was the cause of their first real fight. When they put it up Harry saw his big boob but would never admit it to Sadie. Instead he walked into the room the day after wearing dark sunglasses. It was enough to have Sadie bursting out laughing. Soon Harry was joining in and both of them flopped down on the the couch in convulsions. She remembered Maggie, off to school every Friday but not before she pestered her mum for 'Pennies for the Black Babies'. Not politically correct now but then it was the norm, Maggie would not leave the house that Friday morning until she clutched that big copper penny in her hand to give to Miss McCotter, her teacher, for the African charity. Sadie smiled. She remember Mr Costigan's visit every Friday night collecting her payment or that Bristol cheque she received to purchase Maggie's white First Holy Comunion Dress.

Sadie's nostalgic trip was shattered by the sound of loud, authortive rapping on the door. She was startled for a moment but, composing herself smoothed down her 'peen', buffed her hair in the mirror over the fireplace and answered it.

Hector McNab a small,rotund man in his early fifties, wearing a navy-blue serge suit, black bowler hat and carrying a brown leather brief case strode in without an invitation.

"Good evening, madam," he snapped. "Youse have been holding up this buildin's demolition, do youse know that?" Sadie took a stance.

Folding her arms defiantly she snapped. "At last you've set foot in ma hoose. We hiv been tryin' for years for to get you in

56

here to inspect oor dampness. Noo here ye are threatenin' tae throw us oot."

Hector McNab saw the steam coming from Sadie's ears. But he was not going to be intimidated. He was a hard man an no mere woman was going to get the better of him.

"Youse people are always complaining," he said gruffly.

"Are we supposed tae get pneumonia an' say nothin'?" Sadie retorted.

Hector's eyes swept around the room. "Staunin – er – standin' here I can see no sign of dampness. On the contrary you have a very comfortable home."

"Aye, well just you go intae that bedroom and say that," Sadie snapped.

Hector turned and entered the bedroom. Seconds later he re-emerged. "I see no evidence of dampness in there. In fact the room is tastefully decorated. I like particularly that painting of the mushroom field you have on the wall."

"*That*," Sadie snapped,"is a picture of Celtic Park and there was nae mushrooms on it when we hung it up."

Hector McNab cleared his throat. "Youse are at it!" he said.

"At it, are we?" Sadie was on her high horse. "Let me tell you somethin'. When ma wee Maggie was a wean Ah used tae tuck her intae her wee cot at night. But, unlike other weans, instead o' stickin' a dummy in her mooth, Ah stuck in a snorkel."

Hector threw up his arms. "Oh, woe is me!" he exclaimed.

"Naw, woe is *me*," Sadie said. "When ma auld maw, may she rest in peace," Sadie said, crossing herself, "steyed wi' us, she slept in there. And wance, when it was her birthday, Ah asked her if she would like a nice bed-jaicket? She said naw, she'd rather have a life-jaicket."

"Ah don't believe a' this," Hector said.

"Believe it if ye like. The auld sowel slept in the boattom bunk in there and she was found deid wan moarnin'. It was a shock tae all of us . . . especially efter the post-mortem examination." Sadie stiffened her lip and drew her arms more tightly across her chest.

"So, whit *did* she die of?" Hector asked drearily.

"The Bends," Sadie snapped.

"Well, if the hoose – er – house is so damp why are youse so reluctant for to leave it?" Hector asked.

"Because ma whole life has been in this hoose. A' ma happy memories. Bringin' up the weans, goin' oot tae the midden tae hiv a blether wi' Mrs McWhinnie.the dampness was just a car- buncle. But it could've been eradicated if youse high heid yins would have listened."

Hector McNab was silent for a moment. But he had his duty to perform. This building had to be completely vacated to allow its demolition. He cleared his throat. "Well," he began, "damp or no' damp youse wull have for to vacate these premises by next Tuesday or youse will be forcefully evicted."

The door opened and Harry walked in licking his fingers. Sadie hurried over to him and put her arm through his. "Harry, this is Mr McNab, the factor. He says we've tae be oot by next Tuesday or we'll be evicted."

Harry turned on Hector. "You . . . you . . ." he cried, "would put this wee wumman . . . this wee *pregnant* wumman oot in the street – jist like that?"

Hector spluttered. "*Pregnant!*" he yelled, "Ur you kiddin'? She must be at least *sixty* if she's a day."

"She's a late developer," Harry said.

"*A late developer!*" Hactor cried incredulously.

Sadie nodded."He's right it runs in ma family. *We* were a' late developers in ma family."

"Youse must think Ah came up the Clyde in a bike," Hector snapped.

"Listen," Sadie said, "ma Maw gave birth tae twins when she was eighty-five."

"Ach. ye're haverin', wumman," Hector sniped.

"The twins start school next Monday," Sadie said with a twinkle.

"Enough o' this nonesense," Hector cried. "Youse will be oot o' this hoo – house by next Tuesday or be forceably removed."

"Or *whit*?" Harry snapped.

"Or youse can accept he oaffer of the hoo – house Ah am about for to offer youse. It's your final offer and I have for to tell youse it's wee bit away from the Glasgow city centre."

"Where is it?" Sadie asked her hopes rising.

"Dundee," Hector said flatly.

"*Dundee!*" Harry and Sadie cried in unison.

"The land of *Oor Wullie* and *Fat Boab*," Hector said, a slight smile fleeting across his face.

"Aye, and a fat chance you've got shuntin' us away tae Dundee," Sadie said, dabbing her eye.

Harry saw Sadie's distress. Grabbing Hector by the scruff of the neck, he marched him to the door, flung it open wide and threw the little man out.

"*Oot,*" Harry cried," An' don't come back."

Hector scurried away mumbling. Harry turned and put his arm affectionately round Sadie's shoulders. "There, there," he said.

"Oh, Harry, whit are we gonny dae?" Sadie sobbed.

Harry kissed her cheek. "There, there," he said again, softly, "Don't worry, hen, Ah'll think of somethin'."

Sadie felt assured – only just.

A cup of tea placates all ills and Sadie put the kettle on the gas stove. She poured out her own cup first as Harry liked his cuppa a bit stronger. They sat on the couch in silence for a few moments. Sadie rested her head on Harry's shoulder.

"Who could believe we've been married forty years already?" she purred.

"Aye, life flies in, hen," Harry said.

"Ah don't think that priest wanted tae mairry us," Sadie said, knitting her brows.

Harry laughed. "Father McFungus?" he said, recalling their meeting with the priest the day the arrived at the chapel house to make arangements for their wedding.

"Aye, Father McFungus," Sadie repeated, "Whit a man he was!" she giggled softly.

"We found oot later whit was on his mind, remember?"

Sadie nodded. "Aye, Ah remember that day we went tae see him very well."

Their minds went back to that day more than forty years in the past. They had jumped on a number twenty-nine green 'caur' in the Gallowgate. going from Tollcross to Maryhill. Alighting at Kent Street, where Glasgow's famous *Barras* occupied most of the open territory, they walked up turning into Stevenson Street and Saint Alphonsus' chapel house,

Nervously, they climbed the few stairs up o the large imposing door. A highly polished, gleaming brass bell pull was sited on the red-sandstone wall.

Harry had glanced at Sadie, "Well, here goes," he said and yanked the bell knob. They waited a few seconds and the door was finally opened by a portly lady wearing a heavy black frock.

She eyed the pair up and down with scepticism. "Yes?" she inquired,

"We'd like for to see the priest . . . if he's in," Harry said, stammering just a little.

"Hmm!" Mrs O'Brien, the housekeeper said, narrowing her eyes. She wondered if these two were looking for a handout. Father was much too generous in handing out charity and if it weren't for herself, Mrs O'Brien thought, he'd give the very chapel house itself to some young. homeless couple.

"What would youse be wanting to see him for?" Mrs O'Brien asked in a rich, Irish brogue.

"We want to get married – on the first of November, Sadie squeaked.

"Mrs O'Brien immediately softned. "Oh, you poor dears," she said, "*married!*"

Harry and Sadie nodded. "Aye," they said together.

"Well, ye're lucky," Mrs O'Brien said,"Father McFungus has just come in from a funeral at Dalbeth Cemetery. Makin' arrangements for a weddin' will just be the thing to cheer him up. Come away in."

Mrs O'Brien opened the door wide and Harry and Sadie stepped into the large carpeted hall. Mrs O'Brien showed them into a large room and bade them sit down while she fetched Father McFungus.

They sat together in eerie silence the odour of chintz and Dettol filling their nostrils. They didn't speak, afraid to disturb this holy silence. The cries of the traders just outside, round the corner in Kent Street, was completely muffled by the heavy, dark velour curtains that draped the windows, The silence was suddenly broken by the door flying open and a cheery voice bellowing.

"Hello, hello," the voice boomed as Father Brendan McFungus, a chubby man with a round face that glowed with shiney, rosey cheeks swept in, his hand outstretched. He pumped Harry and Sadie's hands in happy greeting.

"Fa . . . Father McFungus?" Harry stuttered.

"Indeed, indeed," Father McFungus said, "and you are?"

"Ah'm Sadie Broon," Sadie twittered. "We want tae get married."

"On November the first, Ah believe?"

"That's right," Sadie said.

"And who is this idiot?" Father McFungus asked, nodding towards" Harry, who's mouth fell open.

"Ah . . . er . . . Ah'm her financey, Harry McPhatter," he said.

"Youse want to get married, eh? At least that's whit Mrs O'Brien, who's ears have the shape of keyholes says."

"That's right," Sadie said.

"On November the first, that right?" the priest looked over his pinnez.

"We want tae tie the knot." Harry added.

"Roon' yer neck if ye were wise," the priest said, sitting down facing them.

"We love each other," Sadie said.

Father McFungus looked at Harry closely. "When did they let ye oot the asylum?" he asked in a flat tone.

"Ah hiv never been in an asylum," Harry said, startled and annoyed at the remark.

"That's been an oversight on somebody's part," Father McFungus said.

Harry and Sadie glanced quizically at each other.

Father McFungus rose and went over to a huge mahogany sideboard which sat underneath the window. He removed a large diary from the top drawer and re-joined the couple. Opening the pages, he tapped his check with his finger.

"November first ye say?" he murmured.

"Oh, aye, it's got tae be then," Sadie said. "It's ma mammy's birthday and Ah always said Ah' have ma weddin' day on her birthday. She's very sentimental."

"You take efter her, eh," the priest said, "only you are just mental period."

"Ah protest," Harry cried, jumping to his feet.

"An' so ye should," the priest said. "Ah'd protest as well if Ah

61

was gettin' forced into this marriage."

"Ah'm no' gettin' forced," Harry protested.

"November the first, eh?" repeated the priest. "Tell me," he went on, "do you know why November the first is celebrated throughout the world by the catholic church?"

"Er . . . 'Cos it's her maw's birthday?" Harry ventured.

"Don't be stupid," Father McFungus said. "It's because it's All Saints Day . . . know whit that means?"

"Er . . . St Mirren play St Johnstone?" Harry stammered.

Father McFungus looked up at the ceiling in despair. "Ye don't even know the great feast days of the church," he snapped. "Are you sure you're wan o' us?"

"A catholic?" Harry said.

"A human bein'," Father McFungus said flatly.

"Ah've booked the baun', the hall, the taxis and everythin'," Sadie said, "So, y'see it's got for to be November the first."

"And it's got to be in this chapel?" the priest asked.

"Oh, aye," Sadie said, "This is the chapel Harry was baptised in."

Harry nodded. "That's right. In fact Ah think you were the priest that baptised me. Ah was just five days auld, remember – Harry McPhatter?"

"McPhatter – McPhatter," the priest repeated, thinking deeply. Then, snapping his fingers cried, "Och, aye, noo Ah remember. Ye were the ugliest wean Ah's ever seen. At first Ah thought it was April Fool's Day. When Ah gently laid ye doon in the water font Ah remember asking yer maw if she wanted me tae haud yer heid under for five minutes. Look at ye noo, eh? Ye've grown up tae be a big, strappin' ugly man – are you sure you're wan o' ma flock?"

"Well, tae tell you the truth," Harry said, "Ah oaften wonder if there really is somebody up there." Harry gestured with a nod toward Heaven."

"Well." the priest said, "if there is he played a helluva joke on you."

Harry's eyes narrowed. "Whit dae ye mean?" he snapped.

"Aw, do me a favour, son," Father McFungus said, gesturing with his thumb towards Sadie. "Have a look at that coupon"

"Whit aboot it?" Harry said."

"It's like a plate o' tripe," Father said.

"That's no' very nice," Sadie said, hurt.

"Ye've noticed yersel', hen?" Father said facetiously. Then, slapping his thigh, went on. "Tell ye whit Ah'll day, son, Ah don't usually allow dugs intae the church but in your case Ah'll make an exception."

Harry looked blankly at him.

"But Ah don't have a dug," he said.

"Ah always make exceptions for guide dugs and Ah was just being facetious there for to make sure that you really love this – er – girl."

The hesitation was lost on Sadie.

"Oh, yes," Sadie piped up. "he defintely loves me. Ma Maw says Ah'm lucky tae get him".

"Wi' your coupon ye're lucky tae get anybody," the priest retorted."

"Aw, hey," Harry said, "that's beyond a joke."

"Ah, ye *hiv* noticed," Father McFungus said. "Ah thought ye were wearin' rose-coloured specs or is yer eyes just bloodshot?"

Harry ignored the comment. Turning to Sadie, Father McFungus said, "Whit does yer maw say tae ye mairryin' Boris Karloff here.?"

"She says Ah should try and better masel'," Sadie said.

"And so ye should," the priest agreed, " but plastic surgery is very expensive – .and you would need bucketsful o' plastic. For a start ye should get a nose job?"

"Dae ye think Ah should get it turned up a wee bit?" Sadie said, twitching her nose from side to side.

"Na," Father McFungus said, "lookin' at you straight on yer nose looks like two railway tunnels. If ye get it tilted up any mair ye could hing the Mona Lisa on it. Where dae ye buy yer make-up?"

"Boots," Sadie said.

"Ah'd definitely chinge ma supplier," the priest said.

"Where dae ye suggest Ah should go for ma make-up?" Sadie asked innocently.

"B&Q," Father McFungus replied.°

The sarcasm slid over Sadie's head. "Ah've ordered ma weddin' dress," she said dreamily. "It's a white wan."

"Tae go wi' his stick? Father McFungus commented ruefully. Harry looked up. and stared at the priest with just a little anger in his heart.

"Ah do *nut* use a white stick," he snapped. "Ah love Sadie and Ah want tae show ma commitment tae her."

"You should definitely be committed that's for sure," Father McFungas said.

"Ah want tae mairry her and have ma love tested," Harry said,stardust in his eyes.

"Ye should have yer eyes tested," the priest said."Marriage," he went on, "is a commitment you shouldnae go intae wi' yer eyes shut – although in your case Ah'd make an exception. It's no' like *Marks an' Spencer* y'know, where ye can take her back an' chinge her for another model although in your case it could only be an improvement. Whit does yer maw say aboot it son?"

"She said Ah was daft. That Ah was too young and should think twice aboot mairryin' Sadie," Harry said.

"Ah'm surprised that ye even thought *wance* aboot it," the priest said. "Ah mean ye're only a boy."

"Ah'm twenty-two," Harry said.

"Exactly," Father McFungus said, "Just a boy. Ah mean look at her – seventy-four if she's a day."

"Ah'm eighteen," Sadie said quickly.

"Ah wisnae talkin' aboot yer ankle measurement," the priest said.

"Ur you suggestin' that Ah'm fat?" Sadie said angrily.

"Ah would never be so ungallant as to say that to any lassie," Father said."But when ye're leavin', go oot the door sideweys and don't scrape the paint. Noo," he went on, "ye say you've got everythin' organised? Who's supplyin' the caurs?"

"Rollocaurs," Sadie said proudly. The very name sounded imposing.

"Mmmm!" Father McFungus mumbled.

"Dae ye know them, Father?" Harry asked.

"Ah knew them before they chinged their name," Father McFungus said.

"Oh, and whit did they used tae be called?" Sadie asked curiously

"Kamikaze Transport." Father McFungus said, not batting an eye.

Sadie gasped, her hand coming up to her mouth. "Whit dae ye mean, 'Kamikaze'?" she cried.

"Well, Ah'm no' wan to clipe," Father said, "but let's put it this wey. When they were Kamikaze Transport brides used tae leave their hoose a' shining and white an' smellin' o' Chanel Number Five. But by the time they arrived here they were stinkin' o' Castrol XL and oot o' breath."

"*Oot o' breath?*" Sadie cried.

"Aye, shovin' the caur. " Father said.

"Maybe we should chinge oor transport arrangements," Harry volunteered.

"Well unless ye want yer bride tae leave the hoose lookin' like Liz Hurley and arriving here lookin' like Wurzel Gummidge, Ah'd think aboot it."

"Can ye recommend anythin', Father?" Sadie asked, a plea in her voice.

"Call the weddin' aff. It's no' worth it although in your case lookin' like Wurzel Gummidge might be an improvement."

"Oh, we canny call the weddin' aff," Sadie cried.

"Are ye in the club, that it?" enquired Father McFungus.

"Ah am *not* in any club," Sadie said adamantly.

"Whit aboot yer caterin' arrangements)" Father McFungus asked.

"All taken careof," Sadie said matter of factly.

"Oh, and who's doin' that?" Father showed interest.

"Snodges Luxury Weddin's," Sadie said proudly.

"Oh are they back in business again?" the priest asked in surprise.

"Whit dae ye mean, *again?* Sadie asked worriedly.

"Oh Ah thought – och, never mind," the priest dismissed the coversation with a wave of his hand.

"Naw, naw, go on, Father," Harry said, narrowing his eyes.

Father McFungus shrugged. "Ah just thought that efter the mass poisonin' . . ." He didn't get finishing his sentence.

Sadie and Harry jumped to their feet. "*Mass poisonin!*" they blurted out.

"It was nothin'," Father said, "jist a wee weddin' they catered for, hundred and four guests if Ah remember correctly . . . a' rushed tae the Royal Infirmary, groanin' an' moanin'."

"Whit a tragedy!" Sadie said, her mind racing. She flopped back down on to the couch.

"It wisnae too bad, only aboot forty o' them died, Ah think," Father McFungus said with a straight face.

"*Forty* –" Sadie jumped to her feet again.

"Ach but they've probably got it a' sorted oot now," Father said, joining his hands together and looking up to heaven.

"Noo," he went on, "Whit aboot music, eh? Oor organist, Auld Beenie Boal, has been playin' for weddin's here for the past seventy two years. Aye, she's a real raver is Auld Beenie. For two quid she'll gie ye a good rendition of *Abide With Me*. For an extra quid you get three choruses of *The Lord's My Shepherd*. For an extra quid ye get the sheep."

"They're a' funeral hymns," Harry complained.

Father nodded. "Ye're dead right, son. But in your case very appropriate."

Harry decided not not cause a scene.

"Does Auld Beenie dae anythin' else?" Sadie asked. hoping to defuse the anger she couuld see building up in Harry's eyes.

"For a fiver she does a great *Knees Up Mother Brown*," Father McFungus said, doing a jig. "But Ah'm afraid you'd be liable for medical expenses."

"We'll no' bother wi' music," Harry said flatly.

"Ah could whistle while Ah'm performin' the ceremony?" Father McFungus volunteered.

"Furget it," Harry said.

Father McFungus shrugged. "Ah'd play some appropraite records for ye but Ah've run oot o' needles." he said.

"Have ye no' got a compact disc?" Harry asked.

"Naw, just a slipped disc," the priest said. "Ah'm gled Ah don't have tae cairry her ower the threshold. In fact, if Ah was you, Ah'd contact Balfour Beattie and get them tae put her in through the windae. Then, efter five minutes wi' her, Ah'd chuck her oot the windae."

Harry's head became a pressure cooker.Only quick squeeze on his hand from Sadie calmed him down a little.

Father McFungus turned to his diary once more. Browsing

and turning pages, he said. "November first, ye said?"

Sadie and Harry answered rogether. "Aye, the first."

"Right!" Father McFungus said, licking the stub of a pencil he produced and jotting something into the diary. Turning t Sadie, he said, "Just make sure you're well wrapped well, hen, when ye walk doon the aisle. we don't want yer nice, white dress gettin' a' dirty because of the scaffoldin' . . . the roof, y'see."

"Ye're roof's gettin' repaired?" Sadie asked worriedly.

"Naw, we're hopin' tae get wan," Father McFungus said.

That was the proverbial straw that broke the camel's back. Harry jumped to his feet, yanked Sadie off the couch and pulled her towards the door.

"C'mon, hen," he snapped, "Let's get oot o' here. He's done everythin' but divorce us."

Turning at the door, Harry stopped, turned and snapped, "An' Ah don't want you officiatin' at ma funeral."

Mrs O'Brien was almost bowled over as the couple dashed out and into the street.Puzzled, she put her ear to the door of the room Harry and Sadie had just vacated.Father McFungus was dialling a number on the phone. Mrs O'Brien had very good hearing. She heard every. word.

Father McFungus cleared his throat, "Hello," he began, "is that St James' Church of Scotland? Oh, good, can Ah speak to the minister, the Reverend William Robertson? Oh, good, it's yersel', Wullie. Aye it's me. Just checkin', Wullie. Whit was the date again o' that ecumenical golf match? – The *first*? Aye, Ah thought so . . . naw, naw ma diary's free that day. Aye, Ah'll see ye there, Wullie – ta-ta."

Mrs O'Brien peered through the keyhole. Father McFungus was practising his swing holding an imaginary nine iron.

THREE

✿ ✿ ✿

HARRY AND SADIE ROARED WITH LAUGHTER AS THEY RECALLED that day more than forty years ago. Good old Mrs Obrien had given Father McFungus a piece of her mind. For, naturally, her ear had been glued to the door durin the whole time. Father McFungus himself had called at Sadie's house and smoothed things over. Of course he would officiate at her wedding. Of course it was all a mistake. Of course Beenie Boal would play the Wedding March. Of course . . . of course!

Mrs O'Brien explained how the ecumenical golf match was very important to the jolly priest who had a wicked sense of humour.

Harry and Sadie eventually saw the funny side of their encounter with Father Brendan McFungus and the topic had come up many times in company.

Sadie refilled their cups and their laughter subsided to a chuckle. But then the thought of eviction once more crept into Sadie's mind and her depression took over. There was little sleep that night for Sadie. She envied Harry who lay beside her his deep breathing showing he had abandoned the world for a few hours at least. Sadie wondered how he could sleep so soundly when their world was about to crumble about them.

The loud banging on the door made Sadie's eyes open wide. Bright sunlight flooded in through the window. Sadie, startled, dug her elbow in slumbering Harry who was oblivious to the racket.

"Harry . . . Harry.." Sadie cried nervously, "Harry . . . somebody's at the door."

Harry. rubbing the sleep from his eyes, slowly sat up. He yawned widely before the extent of the commotion registered with him. He leapt from the bed followed by Sadie. Staggering, attempting to get into the trousers he had snatched from the

68

chair they were hanging on by the bedside. Sadie was struggling to get into her dressing gown. The banging on the door continued.

"Who's there?" Sadie called but with a good inkling as to who the noise maker was.

"It's Hector McNab," a gruff, authorative voice answered.

"Whit dae ye want?" Harry snapped.

"Ah am here wi' two Sheriff officers for to haund youse a warrant," Hector said in his best dictatorial voice.

"Ah don't care if ye've got Wyatt Earp or Billy the Kid wi' ye," Sadie spat back. "We are *nut* openin' this door." There was a silent pause from the other side of the door followed by hurried whispering.

"Ye canny bribe me wi' a drink," Harry called through the open skylight above the door.

"Ah am not trying for to bribe you wi' a drink," Hector McNab replied.

"Please yersel. then," Harry said.

"Ah am here in ma official capacity and Ah would advise youse wans for to comply or face the consequences."

"Away an' bile yer heid," Sadie rasped.

"Youse canny talk to *me* like that," Hector snapped, standing on top of the shoulders of one of his colleagues. His head poked through the open skylight and he shook his fist.

Sadie immediately fetched her sweeping brush and prodded at Hector's head until he fell backwards landing in the close.

"We are *nut* budgin'," Harry yelled through his cupped hands.

"No until we get a decent oaffer," Sadie added at the top of her voice.

"Youse have had plenty of offers," Hector's voice echoed up the closemouth

"You think ye are somethin' but wait tae you hear frae ma man's uncle," Sadie hollered.

"Oh, Ah'm shakin' at the knees," Hector called in mock terror. "So, who is yer man's uncle?"

"The *Duke of Edinburgh*," Sadie cried. Harry looked at her and they both smiled."

"The Duke of Edinburgh is it?" Hector said. "So that makes youse related tae . . . The . . ."

"That's right," Sadie said, "Harry when did ye last hear frae Auntie Betty?"

"No' since that last Gairden Party," Harry said.

"Youse must think ma heid buttons up the back," Hector said.

"No' yer heid just yer wig," Sadie mocked.

"Ah do not wear a wig," Hector snarled.

"Well, ye're the only man Ah know wi' a Velcro partin'." Harry said.

They could hear Hector coughing and spluttering. "Youse have not heard the last o' this," Hector snapped, "Youse are haudin' up progress."

"And who's haudin' you up, ya wee nyaff," Sadie sniped.

"Ah'll be back," Hector said, "And Ah will not be alone,"

"Aye, well, if ye're comin' back ye'd better bring two sheriffs, a Marshall and a posse alang wi' ye."

"We' . . . we' . . . we'll see," Hector snapped.

Harry and Sadie heard footsteps echo out of the close. They hugged each other in victory. But Harry did not notice the teardrop that fell from Sadie's eye.

The rest of the day went off peacefully with no sign of Hector or the cavalry. Sadie spent part of the morning cleaning the close. Although there were no other tenants in the building certain standards had to be kept up. It was habit anyway and she loved the smell of pine in her nostrils. Harry was reluctant to go out in case Hector McNab and his cohorts should return. Sadie would be nervous if she were to face them alone. But Sadie insisted that he go for his daily donner down to the library in Landressy Street. Since being laid off his work Harry had been looking for something to occupy his time and it was by sheer luck that he bumped into Wee Errol McTavish, in the *Come Inn Pub*, one night shortly after his redundancy. Errol was one of his more artistic buddies. Small and dapper, he had a face that looked like he had done twelve rounds with Mike Tyson. It had more pock marks than the moon's landscape. His appearance belied his name. Wee Errol was named after the famous Errol Flynn. His mother Ina was a great fan of the Hollywood star and always swore that her first child would be called after him. Her husband had argued it was not appropriate for a wean for to be called Errol in their Bridgeton neighbourhood. He would have preferred to call their little son after a good fighting man. A hero from history. But Ina would have none of it. A good living catholic girl she had already made up her mind and had done since the first day she saw her idol on the silver screen.

"If you think ma boy is gonny be called Ghengis," she cried, "Ah'm gonny see the priest. Ah want ma wee boy gied a saints name. There's nae Saint Ghengis."

Wattie, her man, argued there was no St Errol but Ina dismissed his argument with a contemptuous wave, Errol was a saint as far as she was concerned.

And so it was. Wee Errol McTavish was baptised and was soon to be joined by his siblings, Pinocchio, Popeye and Dumbo. Wattie was a great Walt Disney fan. Errol's bludgeoned face was the result of many enounters with those who made fun of his name.t A mere four-feet eight-inches, he could hold his own, but he never forgave his mother for landing him with that tag – neither did the rest of the family. Unable to stand the cruel taunts from school mates, Pinoccio ran away from home and became a nun living a life of quiet contemplation. Sister Pinoccio now runs a school for trick-cyclists, in Zimbabwe.

Harry was glad he had walked into the *Come Inn Pub* the night that was to change his life. Even if it wasn't the night that was to change his life Harry was always glad to walk into the pub.

Wee Errol was seated on a stool at the bar sipping a pint. He caught Harry's eye the minute he entered the pub.

"Harry!" he called in greeting. Errol sounded genuinly delighted to meet him. He remembered the time when Harry got him a job in Glasgow's Pavilion Theatre pantomime *Snow White and the Seven Dwarfs*. He came out at the end of the run to great acclaim. Many had thought he was the best *Snow White* they had seen.

Harry joined him at the bar.

"How's it gaun, china?" Wee Errol said.

Harry shrugged. "Well," he said glumily, "if ye put aside the fact that Ah loast ma joab, Ah'm gettin' throwin' oot ma hoose, ma two weans have vanished somewhere in Canada, Ah canny complain."

"Ye're gettin' thrown oot yer hoose?" Errol commisserated.

"Aye, well, that's the rumour. They say the buildin's tae be demolished."

"Aw, that's a shame," Errol said, "An' whit are ye daein' wi' yersel'?"

"Ah'm sittin' here talkin' tae you," Harry said.

"Naw, Ah meant, how dae ye pass yer time?"

Harry shruggd once more. "The trick is no' tae let things get ye down, Errol. life's philosophy is for to look it straight in the eye, put yer mits up and challenge it wi' every grey cell in yer abdomen. Never let the struggle weaken ye. Stand tall – although in your case Ah admit that would be difficult – dare it. Say, right life, Ah dare ye tae take away ma dignity, ma pride. Put up yer dukes or surrender. 'Cos ye're no' gonny win. Ah'm a man and Ah'm callin' yer bluff. Ah wull never gie in tae this dastardly situation you have seen fit to put me in."

Wee Errol wa silent for a moment then, clearing his throat, said, "So whit are ye daein' noo then?"

"Nuthin'." Harry said.

"Ye should get yersel' a hobby like me, Harry," the wee man said.

"Whit could Ah dae wi' a hobby like you?" Harry asked.

"Naw, Ah don't mean for me tae be yer hobby, Ah loast ma joab in the polis force but Ah didnae let things get me doon. Ah took up a hobby."

"Whit kinda hobby?" Harry showed interest.

"Have ye ever seen artists takin' a big lump of cley an' mouldin' in tae a beautiful sculpture – a heid or somethin'?"

Harry nodded. "Aye, Ah've always admired them people," he said.

"It takes great skill for tae dae that – statues an' a' that," Errol said.

Harry was suitably impressed. "Don't tell me you're wan o' them sculpturers?" he gasped in admiration.

"Naw, Ah dig up the cley for them," Errol said. "It's very rewardin' tae see somethin' you digged up oot the grun suddenly look like a heid. There's no' many get that satisfaction."

"No unless ye're a gravedigger," Harry said.

Errol laughed. "Fancy it?" he asked.

Harry shook his head. "Na," he said, "Ah widnae be any good at that," he said, "Ah've got a sore back. It would kill me."

Errol sadly shook his head. "Aye, well, that would be nae use tae you," he said."But ye *should* come alang tae ma night school, in Bernard Street. Ye might find somethin' that would interest ye.D'ye no' fancy bein' a brain surgeon or somethin'?"

"Naw, that never appealed tae me," Harry said.

"Jist as well, "Errol said, "they don't have that course at ma night school."

Harry was relieved.

"Whit aboot creative writin'," Errol said, snapping his fingers "Mmm! Maybe," Harry said.

"How aboot the *Bible*?" Errol said.

"It's already been written," Harry said.

"Naw, Ah meant, Bible Study," Errol said.

Harry shook his head. "Naw, Ah don't need for tae study the Bible," he said.

"'Cos ye're a Catholic?" Errol said, screwing up his mouth.

"Naw, because Ah've seen every picture Charlton Heston ever made," Harry said

"There must be something ye'd like," Errol said. "Come alang wi' me the morra night. Nae herm hivin' a shufti, eh?"

Harry agreed and Errol left with the intentions of paying a visit to Whitehill Street public baths.

Harry thought about his conversation with Errol all the way home. He told Sadie all about it and she thought it was a great idea.

"Ye should go alang wi' him," she said, "Ye're loast and ye might find somethin' tae interest ye. Ye canny spend the rest o' yer life bein' a couch potato. Ye'll get fat."

Harry had to agree with her. He had already noticed his trousers were getting a bit tight around the waist. His beer intake never occurred to him could well be a contributory factor. He decided there and then that he would go along to Errol's school and see what they had to offer. He was glad they didn't do brain surgery and especially glad that Wee Errol had not signed up for it. He'd stick to asprin.

* * *

Harry had arranged to meet Errol in the *Come Inn Pub* and the wee man was already waiting for him when he arrived.

"Ah, Harry, he said, Ah thought ye might no' turn up."

"How would Ah no' turn up?" Harry asked.

"Well, Ah thought ye might like daein' nuthin'," Errol said. "There's a loat o' folk like daein 'nuthin'. It gies them somethin' tae dae."

"Daein' nuthin' gies them somethin tae dae?" Harry said, trying to see the logic.

Errol nodded. "Right," he said, "Ah've been thinkin' o' other courses ye might be interested in."

"Like whit?" Harry quizzed

"Well, whit aboot widwork? It's really good that."

Harry screwed up his nose. "Hmm. Ah don't know," he said, "Ah'm a – er – conservationist. Ah widnae feel right hackin' away at a livin' organism."

"So, ye're a conservationist, so what?" Errol said, "It's got nuthin' tae dae wi' yer politics. Ah mean hauf o' the class are Labour an there's a couple o' Liberals. Naebody would mind whit ye are."

Harry turned his eyes in despair to Heaven. "It's got nuthin' tae dae wi' politics," he snapped. "Conservationist. Ah am friendly wi' the earth. Ah couldnae staun there and use a chisel on a livin' bit wid."

"The wid's a' deid, Harry," Errol said. "It disnae feel anythin'."

"Ah just widnae feel right. Wance a beautiful tree and there's me gettin' stuck intae it wi' a blade – naw, naw, forget it." Harry vigoursly shook his head.

Wee Errol shrugged. "Well if hittin' a bit o' wid goes against yer grain there's other courses."

"Like whit, for instance?" Harry asked.

"Well," Wee Errol said, "if ye're anywey artistically inclined, there's theatrical make-up."

"Whit's that?" Harry asked.

"It's how for to apply make-up to the actor before his or her performance and then how for to take it aff again when they come aff the stage. – it's a very highly skilled and well-peyed profession."

Harry chewed it over. "Ah suppose," he said, "ye don't have tae be an actor. Ah mean, Ah could help Sadie especially takin' it aff. She screams every night takin' her nail poallish aff."

"How's that?" Errol asked.

"She uses a blowlamp," Harry said with a straight face.

Wee Errol said nothing. He downed his drink. "C'mon," he said, "ye'll see for yersel' whit's on offer."

Harry gulped down what was left of his pint and followed the wee man out onto the street. They headed up towards London Road and jumped on a number nine tram heading for Auchenshuggle, alighting at Marquis Street where they walked down and into Bernard Street.

Wee Errol requested an application form from the registrar, who sat in a side room listening to Victor Sylvester on the radio. Harry let his eyes sweep along the many interesting courses to be had. His eyes settled on *Metalwork*. It appealled to him. He always *was* keen on metal work ever since he saw his father opening a can of McEwans Export.

He was welcomed to the class by Mr Comerford, the teacher, who knew a lot about metal being behind bars for a good part of his old life.

Harry threw himself into his studies with enthusiasm, specialising in bronze He never missed a single class. He was the first at his bench every tutorial night.

Mr Comerford, a tall, gaunt looking man, was delighted with his pupil. He rarely smiled only when he examined Harry's work. Harry's day was made one night when his teacher called him over and asked him if he would go out and get him a fish supper?

He had arrived. Harry had arrived. It was a well known fact that if Mr Comerford asked you to get him a fish supper, you had made it.

Harry hurried with glee down to the chip shop and was brave enough to ask the girl to throw in a a pickle as well.

Sadie was delighted at Harry's obvious enthusiam. Lately, the thought had crossed her mind that she too, might find something interesting at the night school. She could accompany her husband on his educational safaris, but it was decided that it was too dangerous to leave the house empty. They knew that while the house was occupied McNab would have to go through the process of ejecting them. They were not going to make it easy for him.

In the meantime Harry had graduated top of his metalwork class and was known as Charles Bronzan by Mr Comerford.

* * *

Harry and Sadie sat sipping their tea. Their ribs sore with laughing at their meeting with Father Brendan McFungus.

"Ye know," Harry said, "we should have twigged that that priest was a card."

"How were we tae know?" Sadie said.

"Well, mind that first time we went tae Mass there – remember?"

They closed their eyes and re-lived that paricular episode all over again.

Saint Alphonsus Chapel, in the London Road, was a very imposing church built with red stone and standing in London Road adjacent to the famous Glasgow street market, the *Barras*, It had served the people of Calton since 1846. Sadie's mother brought her children up to b regular attenders and was pleased to see them going to daily Mass, and especially Sunday Mass with the school. If she discovered that they had plunked the Sunday ten o'clock service, she would take them aside an tell them in a kindly manner that by avoiding their Sunday duty they were only harming themselves. She had taught them the importance of keeping their spiritual being healthy in this life and so be prepared for the next life. Then she would flatten them.

Harry and Sadie thought they should get acquainted with the church they were to tie themselves together for life. They wanted to see Father Brendan McFungus in action. Everything went well until Father McFungus climbed the stairs of the ornate pulpit to give his sermon.

He stood surveying his congregation before rapping his knuckles and waiting for silence.

"Right," he said, "nae smokin'. Now, it might have come tae your notice that this is not, Ah repeat, *not* an affluent parish. In

76

fact we ur *un*-affluent. Youse have heard of the proverbial church mouse. Oors has chucked it and became a Protestant. Noo, if ye canny keep yer mice happy, youse are in trouble. We are poor. This is because of poor attendances. Just look aboot ye. Youse are on par wi' the attendances at Firhill.

"The only time we get a full hoose here is when there's a funeral. And it's no' because youse are here for to show respect to the deceased. It's in the hope that youse get an invitation for the booze up efter the plantin'. That is not good enough, so it's no'. Well, Ah'm gonny make yer day for ye. Wee Sammy McSorley is being cerried in here the morra prior to his departure. Many of youse wull be surprised that Wee Sammy is being carried in here. Surprised but not shocked because Wee Sammy was usually seen bein' cerried.

"Now for to show youse how miserable youse all are. Ah have been checkin' the collection plate the day – that wan that just went roon youse a' in four minutes flat. Noo, oor collection came to the princely sum of wan pount, twenty-two pence – and two pesatas. Noo, Ah wonder who could have slipped them in, eh? Ah'll be staunin' at that door as youse file oot efter Mass and God help the wan wi' the best tan.

"And look at this gear Ah'm wearin'. Oor drama club have oaffered me the part o' Wurzel Gummidge in their next prodution. Ah'm ashamed tae be seen walkin' intae God's hoose lookin' like this. In fact Ah'm ashamed tae be seen walkin' intae a *Public* hoose lookin' like this.

"Last Sunday the collection plate went roon an no' only did we get nae money. We didnae even get the plate back. Somebody in this chapel is eatin' their fish an' chips aff a widden plate. Ah can only hope that God forgives them and they get a skelf in their gums. Another thing, for ages Ah have been complainin' aboot the roof. We really should have wan. Hauf oor congregation have got arthritis – and they're the weans.

"The other hauf have deserted us tae join another denomination. *Not* because they want tae become Protestants. Naw, it's because that other crowd have central heatin'. Ah feel ashamed when Ah see their congregation queuin up on a Sunday, packin' oot that church. A' dressed up tae the nineties. The wimmen in their fur coats a' smellin' o' lavender. The men in the blue serge suits smellin' o' *Old Spice*. You men smell o' *Old Socks*. Ah have deduced that fur us tae get up alangside o' them, we wull have to have an extra 202 funerals. We really dae need mair funds and Ah would ask youse tae dig intae yer poackets. There are many other things oor chapel needs. For instance an organ. Maist organs rise up oot the flair. *Oors* fell right through the flair. Ah always maintain that was retribution. Wee Maisie had nae right comin' up through the flair playin' *Tico Tico*. Ah do not blame the woodworm on the floorboards. They've got tae live. So Ah hope youse have been listenin' and those of you who are sober, will stand now, we will sing hymn number twelve thousand and wan, *I am comin' down to bless you noo the lift is workin*. We will be accompanied by Wee Ina on the spoons."

Harry and Sadie doubled up, holding their sides as they recalled Father McFungus's sermon that day.

"We should've known he was a wag," Harry said.

"Ah thought he was serious," Sadie replied. "Anywey, everythin' turned oot well in the end."

Harry agreed. "Aye, he was some man," he said.

"He didnae have you jiltin' me anywey," Sadie said, pecking Harry's cheek.

"Aye, and he definitely did come up trumps on oor weddin' day, remember?" Harry said, chuckling.

"Aye, and there was nae scaffoldin'," Sadie laughed. "Jist wan thing Ah was a wee bit annoyed aboot," she added, "was when Ah walked doon the aise. Insted o' Auld Beenie Boal playing *Here Come The Bride*, he had Bing Crosby singin' *Straight Down the Middle*."

"Aye, he was golf daft," Harry said. "Ah'll bet that big letter *G* on his vestment didnae staun' for God."

"Well, he's still goin' strong, still there. Ah thought he'd be the Pope by this time," Sadie said.

"He must be a good age noo," Harry commented.

"No' that auld, Harry," Said said. "He wisnae that auld really when we first went tae see him forty years ago."

Harry shrugged. "Maybe ye're right," he said.

"It's a' right laughin', Harry", Sadie said, becoming serious once more, "but whit are we gonny dae?"

"Well, Ah suppose we could buy a twenty-eight inch television set," Harry said.

"We've got a big TV set," Sadie said.

"It's the boax Ah want. We could station it under the Kingston Bridge and be as snug as two bugs in a rug," Harry quipped.

"It's no' funny," Sadie said. "Ah don't fancy sleepin' under the Kingston Bridge, a' that traffic flying overhead."

"Ye frightened a big double decker fa's on toap o' ye?" Harry said.

"Naw, Ah'm frightened the bridge fa's on toap o' me," Sadie said. "An' stoap yer kiddin'," she added.

"Oh, Ah don't know," Harry said whimsically, "Just think, wi' yer ain boax ye could choose where ye want tae stey. We could plant it in Newton Mearns and have a very desirable addresss."

"Aw. Harry." Sadie said, snuggling up to her husband, "If we move intae a boax, Ah'd miss ma electric blanket".

"Ach, ye've still got me, hen," Harry said.

"Lets have another wee drink. It *is* oor Ruby Anniversary efter a'," Sadie said.

Harry rose and went over to the table, then to the sideboard. He turned and shrugged. "There's nothin' left, hen. We'll just have tae drink mulk."

"Not on yer life!" Sadie said, "Away doon tae Abdul Singh's shoap and get a boattle. Try and walk past the *Come Inn*, eh?"

Sadie went into her purse, pulled out a twenty-pound note and handed it to Harry. She patted him affectionately on the cheek.

Harry put the note into his wallet which he stuck in his hip pocket.

* * *

The *Come Inn Pub* was swinging as Harry approached. He walked on but the smell of the beer and the raucous singing coming from the hostelry made him turn.

"One pint wouldn't do any harm," he reckoned.

It was karaoke time and the pub was jammed. A man, with upturned lip was on the platform gyrating and attempting to sound like Elvis.

"Ah, it's yersel', Harry," Erchie the barman said. "Usual?"

Harry nodded and Erchie pulled him a pint and shoved it across the bar.

"Don't usually see you in the night, Harry," Erchie said.

"Sadie an' me ran oot o' a wee refreshment and Ah'm goin' doon tae Abdul's for a boattle," Harry said, wiping froth from his mouth with the back of his hand."

"Ah mean it *is* oor anniversary efter a',"he added.

"Here, have that – on the hoose," Erchie pushed over a large Glenmorange.

"Thanks, Erchie," Harry said, raising his glass."

"How about a song, Harry?" Erchie said, "You're a good chanter. C'Mon."

Harry shuffled his feet and dropped his head in mock embarrassment. "Aw," he said, "Ah'd need tae oil ma thrapple first."

"Ah thought ye might," Erchie said, shoving over another malt whisky.

Harry downed the drink and ceared his throat. Erchie battered the top of the bar with his fist. "Order please . . . order. We have here oor ain Luciano Havyertottie who wull now sing for us."

"Ah wanna hear Elvis," a wee drunk man in a Mets baseball cap cried.

Harry ignored him and burst into "*Please release me – .*" He ended to wild applause.

"Ah wanna hear Elvis," the wee drunk repeated, staggering against a table and knocking a man's pint over. The drinker jumped to his feet and grabbed the drunk by the throat. But, before he could throttle the wee man, Erchie was over like a shot, separating them.

"Noo, nae fightin'," he said, " Ah'll replace yer drink, pal."

That was enough to placate he big man who released the drunk with a contemptable shove.

"Ah wanna hear Elvis," the drunk repeated. It was Erchie's turn to brab him by the throat. Holding him at arms length, he said. "Listen you. No' only wull ye *hear* Elvis. Ye'll have the pleasure o' *meetin'* him, face-to-face if ye don't shut up."

The man mumbled something and staggered away to sit in a corner. With one defiant call he yelled "Ah wanna hear Elvis." Erchie gave him a dismissive wave and smiled to himself.

Harry didn't feel the deft hand slip into his hip pocket as he stood at the bar. Nor did anyone notice Harry's wallet suddenly vanish into Elvis Pressley's sequined pocket. Harry bade Erchie goodnight and stepped into the street. Abdul's shop was, appropriately, at the corner.

Abdul Singh greeted Harry with a cheery wave of his hand. "Ah, good evening sahib," he said in a mock, accentuated Indian accent.

"Aye, hello," Harry said.

Abdul was a roly-poly man who, when he smiled, flashed a picture of highly polished carerra marble. "You want something?" the teeth flashed.

"Aye, Ah'd like a boattle of Bells Mr – er – Mr – er –" Harry stammered.

"Singh," Abdul said, "Singh."

Harry shrugged. "Okay," he said, and, throwing open wide his arms, sang, "*Ah would like a boattle of Bells whisky*."

Abdul laughed loudly, "Naw, naw," he said, "my name is *Singh* – Abdul Singh."

Harry blushed, "Oh!" he said.

Abdul shook his head. "Sorry," he said, "nae Bells – just Jack Daniels."

Harry shook *his* head. "Naw, naw," he said. "Ah make it a point for no' tae drink anythin' that's called efter a man's name. It's ma principle."

"Principle's are very good things," Abdul said, "but you asked for Bells – surely that's called after a *Sahib Bells*, eh?"

"Maybe, maybe no'," Harry said.

"Well would sahib like something called efter a bird?"

"Like whit?" Harry asked.

"*Grouse* eh – no' Marylyn Monroe," Abdul laughed.

"Naw, gie me a boattle o' Johnny Walker," Harry said.

Abdul made no comment on Harry's forgetting his principles.

Pushing over the bottle, he said. "That is very good Scotch, so it is."

"A' Scotch is good," Harry said, "But whit would you know. Ah mean you're main drink must be tea – if ye really dae come frae India."

Abdul's chest inflated and he drew himself to his full height. "I am a true Indian *and* a true Scotsman," he snapped.

"If you're a Scotsman whit does that make me then?" Harry said.

"A twit," Abdul said.

"Ah am a *true* Scotsman," Harry said, "Ah was born under the shadow of that great Scottish temple."

"The Gorbals mosque?" Abdul said with raised eyebrows.

"Celtic Park," Harry corrected.

"Ah, fitba!" Abdul sighed, "the great religion."

"Where dae ye come frae?" Harry asked.

"Frae here," Abdul said.

"Naw, Ah mean originally?" Harry said.

"Frae Govan. We flitted tae here tae be near the shoap," Abdul said, falling into the Glasgow patois.

"Naw, Ah mean – where did yer ancestors come frae?" Harry pressed.

"Ah," Abdul said, "My great Grandfather, was jailed sittin' astride an elephant and leadin' a whole herd o' them shoutin' "Down wi' the British Raj – he was a rebel."

"Aye, and an idiot," Harry said, "Ye just didnae lead a herd o' elephants doon the street in the Punjab shoutin' abuse at the British durin' their Raj in the nineteenth century."

"This happened in Sauchiehall Street just last week," Abdul said.

"Well, it disnae matter," Harry said, "Nooadays that is called Road Raj – Ha-Ha, get it?" Harry guffawed.

Abdul stood stoney faced.

"Ah am surprised that your auld gran'faither would subject they elephants tae such indignity. Ah mean youse are an animal-lovin' people, int ye? Youse do nut eat beef, Ah believe?"

"That is correct," Abdul agreed.

"Whit dae youse dae wi' yer coos, then?" Harry asked.

"Ah, the coos!" Abdul sighed, "they are sacred. When I was a wee boy ma faither took me to the old country for a wee holiday. There, from my windae, Ah could sit and watch the cows wander aboot the street unhindered."

"Harry shrugged. "Ye can dae that here if ye stey in Blythswood Square," he said.

"Know whit Ah think?" Abdul said, "I think you are a racist."

"Ah have been known for to frequent the Shawfield dugs." Harry replied.

"And you are definitely not P.C." Abdul added.

"Ah, ye've got me there," Harry said, "Ah know nuthin' aboot personal computers, that's true."

"Ah mean you are *not* politically correct," Abdul corrected.

"Ah am so, " Harry said, "Ah've voted Labour a' ma life. Ye canny be mair politically correct than that,"

Abdul threw up his arms. "Enough of this chit-chat," he said. "That will be twenty pounds for the whisky. We're on a special."

"That's a lotta rupees," Harry said.

"Ah widnae know aboot that," Abdul said, "Ah don't even know what a rupee looks like."

"Are you sure you're a real Asian and no' jist kiddin' on – jumpin' on the bandwaggon 'cos that race has a very good reputation – steyin' open a' 'oors an' that?"

"Well, Ah'm no' frae Ballykissangel," Abdul said. Then, pointing to his face, added, "Whit dae ye think this is – *Ambre Solaire?*"

"Right, so whit dae you know aboot Scottish culture, an' that?" Harry said.

"Oh, goodness gracious me!" Abdul said, throwing up his arms, "I am fully interrogated into Scottish culture. I know all the great Scottish songs. I could be another Sahib Sidney Devine."

"Ach, away ye go,"Harry said. "Whit Scots songs dae ye know?"

Abdul cleared his throat. "Listen," he said and burst into song:

"*Wi'a tandoorie on his bonnet, a red tandoori onit,*" he began, followed by, "*By yon Bhoona Banks and by yon Bhoona Braes.*" Abdul was on full hrottle now, "*Aw for Bonnie Biryani Laurie, I would lay me doon and dee.* See," he said, finishing with a flourish. "I am fully interrogated. Real Glesca, that's me," he said proudly.

"Ach yer granny's up a gum treee," Harry said.

"That's another thing," Abdul said. "Youse have called your grannies efter oor, good Indian breid – Nan."

"Away ye go," Harry said.

"I know yer great poet – Rabbi Burns." Abdul said with pride, "Listen," Abdul put his hand to his heart and began to recite, "*Great chieftain o' the puddin' race, come in this minute and wash yer face* and *Wee coorin' timorous beastie, for ma cat you'll make a feasty*. How about that, then, eh? Och aye the noo," Abdul smiled. his teeth lighting up the shop.

"That disnae make ye a Scot," Harry scoffed.

"I have tried for to get a kilt in the Abdul tartan but there's none," the shopkeeper said, disappointed. "Still, I went for the next best thing."

"And whit was that?" Harry asked.

"The Currie tartan, whit else?" Abdul said.

Harry laughed. "Right, Ah'll pey ye for ma whisky," He said, dipping his hand into his hip pocket.

He pulled his hand out quickly and frantically looked about the floor at his feet.

"Ma wallet!" he wailed, "Ah've loast ma wallet."

Abdul threw up his arms.

"If you have loast your wallet I'm Gunga Din."

"Ye'll need tae gie me tick," Harry said.

"Tick Ah don't gie, Tikka Ah do gie," Abdul said, lifting the bottle and putting it under the counter.

"Aw, go on, Mr Singh," Harry pleaded.

"Ma name is not Abdul Oxfam," Abdul said bluntly. "Here, he added, handing Harry a popppdom, "Chew on that. Very good for calming nerves – and boy, have you got a nerve."

"Whit is it?" Harry asked, examining the delicacy. "It looks like something ye'd find in a field full o' coos."

"You have a fixation aboot coos, man," Abdul said. "Say nothing bad aboot coos. A coo could be the reincarnation of your mother-in-law. So, show respect."

Harry shook his head "Naw, naw, ma mother-in-law wull come back as Jack the Ripper."

"You are very funny man for twit who has lost his wallet," Abdul said.

"Sadie wll kill me," Harry said, "It was her money."

"Oh, your wife is Mrs Sadie frae the buildin' they're gonny pull down, eh?"

84

Harry nodded.

"She a good customer," Abdul said, beaming. "She put bandage on my wee Shereen's knee when she fell off her bicycle. She's a good wumman."

"Aye, she is," Harry said with feeling.

"Here, have yer bottle and this chappati and pey me later," Abdul said, "ma special offer this week. 'Be happy wi' a chappati' and this goes wi' it, too – a C.D. of Sydney Devine singin' *Tiny Bubbles.*"

Harry shook his head. "We've got a record o' Sydney Devine singin 'Tiny Bubbles'," he said.

"In Hindi?" Abdul asked.

"There are many songs in life that jogs memories. That wan reminds me o' ma wee dug Mitzi," Harry said.

"Your dug could sing Tiny Bubbles?" Abdul raised his eyebrows.

"Naw, naw, it makes me think o' the day when Sadie bought the record roon' the Barras. She brought it in and we put it on right away. Aye, Ah remember that day tae this."

"What's that got to do wi' your wee dug?"

"As soon as we put the record on Wee Mitzi gave a howl and dashed right through the door. We hivnae seen her tae this day," Harry sadly shook his head. Wan minute Wee Mitzi was sittin' there, like the dug in His Master's Voice, listenin' tae Tiny Bubbles and the next she was gone."

"Whit a shame!" Abdul said, "Ah love wee dugs masel'."

"Tae make matters worse," Harry went on, "the door was shut at the time."

"So no' only did you have to get a new dug, you had to get yer sels a new door?" Abdul commiserated.

"Naw, Mitzi could never be replaced. But Ah had tae get a new door, for Sadie's sake. Ah was thinkin' o' her staunin' there in her underwear wi' nae door."

"Whit made ye think of Sadie standin' there in her underwear," Abdul asked

"Because Ah'm always thinkin' aboot Sadie staunin' there in her underwear," Harry said.

"Ah'm always thinkin' the same," Abdul said.

"*Whit*!" Harry snapped, "*You* are always thinkin' aboot ma

85

Sadie staunin' there in her underwear?"

"Naw, naw," Abdul said, shaking his head vigorously. "Ah think aboot ma wee wife, Biddy, staunin' there in her underwear."

"Biddy?" Harry queried. "That's anusual name for an Asian wumman, is it no'?

Abdul nodded, "She grew up in poverty and became a communist when she was very young and, in the streets of Bombay, became known as Red Biddy."

"Aw!" Harry said as though he understood.

"Anyway." Abdul said, "Tell Sadie ma wee Shereen's knee is a'right."

"That's if Ah get a chance tae talk," Harry said, "Efter a' Ah've lost the money she gave me. So, if ye see a wee dug runnin' intae yer shoap don't kick it oot."

"How no'?" Abdul asked.

"It might be me," Harry said with a smile.

Abdul laughed loudly as Harry left clutching his bottle.

Things were still swinging as he passed the *Come Inn Pub*. He hesitated, then turning entered. The singer on the platform was singing in Swahili or so it sounded. No, Erchie had not found his wallet but would keep an eye open when he was cleaning up. He commiserated with Harry and pushed over another whisky on the house. Harry left the singer bawling and headed home to face Sadie and all their problems.

★   ★   ★

Sadie was sitting waiting when Harry arrived home. She wondered what was keeping her husband – but had a good guess. She'd sat in silence since Harry left, not even switching on the radio or television. Normally the sound of life would echo round her building. For most of her life, twenty-seven Glenvernon Street was more than just a bulding. It was the centre of the universe. Up that close was all of humanity. Old Mrs Bell on the second floor was the communal midwife. As soon as baby started to arrive the cry went out to fetch Old Peggy Bell. Trouble? Get Wee Sammy McKenzie, on the first floor. Sammy was the Perry Mason of the street. He had the 'gift of the gab' and always reckoned he was meant for the bar. But the only bar he was meant for was the one in the Come Inn, where he was a regular. He *did* represent Bing Broon, so called because of his winged ears and not his voice, at the Glasgow Sheriff Court when Bing was accused of breaking into Margaret Forrester's shop, in London Road, and despite Bing being caught red-handed carryin' four sequined ballroon dresses as he walked down nearby Bain Street, he got him off with a two-year stretch in Barlinnie. Although some said that the sheriff had been contemplating putting Bing on probation. Bing had explained that he was taking the dresses to the 'steamie' in Gibson Street before presenting them to the one-legged club for their annual dance.

For all that, Sammy was considered the street's top lawman. Some referred to him as the K.C. – Kid Cavalry – always coming to the rescue in the nick of time to save somebody doing time in the nick.

There was always the tap-dancing in the close of wee Michelle McGeachie who just could not keep still.

Michelle's mother, Senga, had once seen Shirley Temple and Mickey Rooney dancing across the silver screen and she was hooked. She swore that her first child would be a hoofer, a Hollywood star just like her favourite screen idol, and although wee Michelle did love tap dancing, she was a bit cheesed off going around the Calton dressed like Mickey Rooney. Senga, too, was always tapping.

Still, the noise of those happy, dancing feet in the close was a joy to Sadie. It not only meant a vibrancy up her close but it meant *young* life. When that last furniture van turned the corner it took more than wardrobes and sideboards with it. It took Sadie's life. These thoughts were going through her mind during Harry's absence.

Here was her wedding anniversary, her fortieth, and she sat alone. Not a single sound in the building except for the odd stray cat who had undoubtedly spotted a scavenging rat. She wondered what had happened to Norman? She worried about Norman. Even as a child it was obvious to all that he was a prodigy – although he didn't like discussing his religion. Like Senga McGeachie she had high, high hopes for her son. She could see Norman being snapped up by some astute Hollywood or televison producer. Many folk could blow smoke down their nose but Norman could send jets of thick smoke out of his ears. People looked on in wonder for Norman didn't smoke.

She suddenly wished Harry would hurry up as she knew she was about to burst into tears. The thought had hardly passed through her mind when Harry walked in carrying his bottle.

"Think Ah got loast?" he said.

"Ah was just sittin' here thinkin'," Sadie said.

Harry poured out two whiskies, handed one to Sadie and joined her on the couch at the fireside,

"Whit were ye thinkin' aboot?" Harry said.

"Whit dae ye think?" Sadie said, giving him a'look'.

"Ah keep tellin' ye eveythin' will turn oot a'right," Harry reassured her.

"Ah worry," Sadie said, "and Ah was wonderin' aboot the weans? Did Norman become a big star like Ah always thought he would?"

"Ah know that's why ye keep watchin' the David Attenborough show," Harry said. "But ye need mair talent that jist blawin' smoke oot yer ears, Sadie."

"Norman could also throw his voice, Harry," Sadie said with pride. "Mind the time we were up the stairs at Auld Mrs Bell's on the second floor, celebratin' her man's release. Everybody was daein' their party piece and everybody said 'Shhh' 'cos we could hear Norman's voice sayin' *help, help!* and he wisnae tae be seen in the room. Everybody was mesmerised and then we saw him ootside in the street. Everybody applauded."

"Sadie, he'd fell oot the windae," Harry said.

"It disnae matter," Sadie retorted. She would have nobody doubting her son's theatrical prowess.

Harry and Sadie sat up most of the night reminiscing. Tomorrow was another day. Would Hector McNab arrive with a posse? Could they be be forcefully evicted? How would they get all their furniture into a Hitachi box? These thoughts flooded Sadie's mind as she put her head on the pillow. She turned to ask Harry what the answer to those questions was? Harry was in deep slumber. Sadie wished she had his peace of mind.

Sadie awoke with a start. She felt the gentle shaking of Harry's hand on her shoulder. She looked up. Harry stood at the bedside holding a cup of tea.

"Cupa tea, hen?" he said.

Sadie propped her self up and gratefully took he cup and saucer. She sipped the hot, sweet tea, smacked her lips and said. "Oh, that's lovely! Ye canny beat a wee cuppa tea."

"How're ye feelin'?" Harry said.

" Better than Ah should," Sadie said.

"Well, you just have a long lie, hen," Harry said.

"Naw, Ah canny," Sadie said. "Ah'll have tae tidy up."

"Whit ye want tae tidy up for when we're getting slung oot."

"Ah don't care. Ah hate an untidy hoose," Sadie said, finishing off her tea and putting the cup on to the bedside cabinet.

"Well, Ah think ye're daft," Harry said, "but Ah know you."

Sadie swung her legs out of the bed and dressed hurriedly. "Dae ye think we should barricade the door?" she asked Harry, who was sitting reading a book on working in bronze.

"Maybe," he said, not looking up.

"Ah'm just waitin' on that door goin' any minute and that wee bachle, Hector McNab staunin' there," Sadie grimaced. "Y'know, Ah dreamt aboot him. The door went and when Ah opened it he was staunin' there in a Gestapo uniform. He gave a nazi salute, clicked his heels and said, 'Ve Haff vays of making you valk'." Sadie put on a clipped, German accent.

Harry laughed. "Aye, well, he'll need a whole panzer division wi' him if he does show up," he said.

Tomorrow was Tuesday – deadline day.

"Whit will we dae wi' oor furniture? Sadie asked worriedly.

"Whit dae ye mean?" Harry said.

"Well, ye canny get it intae a cardboard boax," Sadie said.

"Ach, Ah was only kiddin' aboot that," Harry laughed.

"Where are we gonny go?" Sadie said, hiding a tear.

"Maybe yer faither wull put us up for a while," Harry said.

Sadie shook her head. "Naw," she said, "Remember he took that big blonde's cat in when he found it injured?"

"Whit's that got tae dae wi' it?" Harry asked drawing his eyebrows down.

"Well, he took her in as well," Sadie said. "Ah ever telt ye in case ye thought he was a dirty auld man."

"He always was a cat lover," Harry said with a wry smile.

"It means he'll have nae room for us," Sadie said.

Harry agreed. Besides, being a man of the world, he wouldn't want to cramp the old man's style

Sadie pulled over an easy chair and placed it at the door.

"Ye don't think that that'll deter Hector McNab, dae ye?" Harry scoffed.

"Naw, but Ah just feel mair secure wi' that here," Sadie said."Anywey," she added, "Ah'm no' openin' the door."

"Maybe he'll open it for ye," Harry said.

Before Sadie could reply here was a loud rap at the door.

Sadie gasped, her hand coming up to her mouth. "Who could that be?" she stamered.

"Only wan wey tae find oot," Harry said, pulling the chair away.

"Oh, don't dae that," Sadie wailed.

"How dae Ah open the door, then? Harry protested.

"Don't open it," Sadie said, shaking.

The squeaky voice of Minnie Magee wafted through the sky-light. "Mrs McPhatter – er – Sadie – it's me, Minnie."

Sadie and Harry glanced at each other. Harry smiled.

"Whit is it Minnie?" Sadie said.

"I have something for you," Minnie said in her poshest voice.

"Er – we've got the door barricaded in case Hector McNab shows up," Sadie said.

"Quite right!" Minnie said. "But please let me in."

"Can ye no' through it through the open skylight, whatever it is?" Sadie cried.

"I would rather give it to you personally," Minnie said. "Besides I want to get off the street – a man has been following me."

"Did he get a swatch at yer knees?" Harry said facetiously.

"I don't know. I just know when I walked down London Road he was there and when I turned into Claythorn Street he was there and then, when I turned into Stevenson Street, there he was again."

"Are ye sure he was followin' ye, Minnie?" Sadie asked scep-tically.

"Oh, yes, most definitely," Minnie was positive.

"Whit did he look like?" Sadie asked.

"Oh, he was a wee man wearin' dugarees and pushing a big sweeping brush and lifting stuff with a shovel and putting in in a cart."

"Were ye frightened he was gonny sweep ye aff yer feet?" Harry said, laughing.

"You can't be too careful," Minnie said, "especially when you know the affect you have on men, even *wee* men."

Sadie opened the door. "Come away in, Minnie," she sad.

Minnie entered and Sadie steered her to the couch. Minnie sat down and, settling down, pulled up her skirt just a little to show her knees.

"You would really need a strong, resolute man to be on hand here to protect you fom Hitler McNab," Minnie said, narrowing her eyes at the thought.

"Hey, Ah'm here," Harry cried.

"But you're too gentle a person, Mr McPhatter, you would need someone like – like – er – James Bond. If James Bond were here right now Hector McNab would have no chance."

"Neigher would James Bond," Harry said with a grin.

"Whit was it ye wanted tae gie me, Minnie?" Sadie asked curiously.

"This," Minnie said, pulling out a picture from her bag and handing it to Sadie.

Sadie studied the picture, her brows knitting. "Who is it?" she asked.

"That," Minnie said, "is Saint Wimpey."

Sadie glanced at Harry who shrugged. Turning back to Minnie, she said.

"Who is St Wimpey?"

"He is the patron saint of houses," Minnie said, a satisfied look on her face. "One prayer to Saint Wimpey and all your housing problems will be over. My Horace used to swear by Saint Wimpey. In fact, in the morning when we got up and Horace was saying his morning prayers, he would look at me and swear."

"Ah could believe that," Harry said. " But Ah know maist o' oor saints and Ah hivnae heard o' a Saint Wimpey. If Ah pray

91

tae Saint Wimpey as sure as hell we'll no' get a hoose – probably a hamburger."

"No, no," Minnie said, " I knew you were religious people and that's why I thought you would appreciate this little picture."

"And that was very kind of ye, Minnie," Sadie said, patting her on the shoulder.

"Yes, well," Minnie said, rising, "don't you give in. Stick to your guns."

"Ye hivnae got a picture o' Saint Barratt, have ye?" Harry piped up.

Minnie shook her head. "No, just you have a word with Saint Wimpey there. He's just a wee brick, so he is."

"Well, he would be, wouldn't he?" Harry grinned.

"I really must go now, Minnie said turning towards the door.

The minute Minnie left Harry swung the couch over to block the door.

"Ah've never heard o' a Saint Wimpey," Sadie said.

"Who has?" Harry said.

"Ah mean, look at that picture," Sadie said, handing up the picture.

"Whit saint ever looked like that?" she added.

Harry studied the picture which showed a man wearing a golden mitre, dressed in sackcloth and carrying a hod.

"Can he be real?" Sadie said, screwing up her nose.

"Of coorse no'," Harry said, "She's painted this hersel' ".

"But why?" Sadie asked, puzzled.

"Psychological," Harry said. "She knows you're a religious wee wumman and the thought that ther's a patron saint of hooses might gie ye some hope. He's no' real, Sadie."

"Neither is she," Sadie said, "but her heart's in the right place."

"Aye," Harry said. Sadie put the kettle on.

For the rest of the day they sat in tenterhooks awaiting a knock on the door. When nothing happened they began to relax a bit and sat down on the couch by the fire. They sat listening to the silence.

"Quiet intit?" Sadie commented. Harry nodded. He leaned over and switched on the television set. The programme's introductory music boomed out and the title flashed up on the screen – *Neighbours.*

"Switch that aff," Sadie snapped.

Harry switched the set off and they sat in silence for moment. Sadie shivered as the fire began to subside. She looked at Harry who immediately rose and attacked the huge coal lump in the bunker with a heavy blow of the hammer. He scooped up a shovelful of coal and heaped it on to the fire. The coal had dampened down the flames and Sadie shivered pulling her cardigan tightly around her body.

"It'll catch in a minute, hen," Harry said, rubbing his hand down Sadie's arm.

She smiled. "Ah'm feelin' a bit peckish," she said, rubbing her own arm.

"Feel like a fish supper?" Harry said, the thought making his own mouthwater.

"Do Ah no' just!," Sadie said.

"Ah'll nip doon tae Mario's," Harry said.

"Tell Mario tae put in an ingin," Sadie called as Harry vanished out of the door.

Harry's nose twitched as he headed down London Road. The succulent and tantalising aroma of fish and chips wafted along the street guiding hungry souls to a luscious, mouth-watering banquet.

Mario Valente's fish suppers were fit to lay on a royal tableΛ Harry was greeted as he entered the shop. It was early evening and things were quiet. Mario, a round. jolly man, threw up his arms. "Ah, Harry Mac-a-Phatter! How-are-ye?"

Harry shrugged. "So-so," he said.

"Aye, Ah hear-o' yere-a troubles" Mario said. "You no'-a go where the big-a heid yins want-a ye tae go, eh?

"Whit's wrang wi' that?" Harry said.

"You're a nice-a man, Harry, but you're-a too-a fussy," Mario said.

"Whit dae ye mean?" Harry said, annoyed.

"Well," Mario went on."I -a like your-a custom, Harry. And wee Sadie's tae. Noo, Sadie come-a in and asks for a fish-a supper jist-a like that. But you come in and-a want tae know everything boot the fish-a supper. Too fussy. So, why-a you no like-a the hooses oaffered ta youse, eh? Let them pull the buildin' doon and we a' get-a peace na mair-a weans breakin' the windaes o' a' the empty hooses."

"Ah don't know where ye get the idea that Ah'm too fussy," Harry complained. "Ah'm the maist unfussy guy in the world."

"A'right," Mario said, "So, whit you want, eh?"

"Two fish suppers,"

"Right,", Mario said, turning to his vat of fat.

"Is yer fat at the right temperature?" Harry said.

Mario threw up his hands.

"It's-a bilin'," he said."Ye'll hear the wee totties screamin' as they a dive in, a'right?"

"Ah'll take your word for it," Harry said. "Ah hope ye've cut the chips two and wan-eighth inches long," he added.

Mario turned, slapped the top of the counter with the palm of his hand. He took a wooden ruler from a drawer and slapped it down in front of Harry.

"Dae ye want a spirit level?" he said." Jist tae make-a sure ma chips are straight."

"Ah'll take yer word for it," Harry said.

Mario spread a scoop of chips on to the paper.

"You want-a salt and vinegar?" he asked.

"Is it sea salt?" Harry asked.

"It is," Mario said, sprinkling on the salt.

"That's awful daurk lookin' salt," Harry said.

"It's-a frae the Black-a Sea," Mario said, stoney-faced.

"Where dae ye get yer totties frae?" Harry asked, taking a chip and popping it into his mouth. "Ah prefer Ayrshires," he added sucking in cold air and waving his hand in front of his burning mouth.

Mario took a potato from a sack, thumped it down on the counter and pointing a finger at it, addressed it.

"Where dae you-a come frae, wee tottie?" he asked sternly. And then, from the side of his mouth, said, "I'm-a from Ayrshire where Rabbie comes-a frae. Right, ye've got it straight frae the tottie's mooth," he said. "See it's eyes light up."

Harry had a twinkle in his eye. He was winding Mario up and chuckling to himself. Mario was a good sport and the banter was just a bit of fun.

94

"Very good Mario," he said. He decided to keep it up. "How aboot some ascetic acid?"

"Whit-a that?"

"Vinegar," Harry said.

"Why you no' say-a vinegar like everybody else?" Mario moaned.

"Nane o' yer sauce," Harry said.

"Hivnae got-a sauce," Mario said "Jist-a vinegar."

"Throw in an ingin, wull ye?"

Mario scooped out a pickled onion from a large jar and placed it on the grease-proofed paper.

"That-a ingin came-a frae Spain," he said. "Ah ordered it-a specially for you. It's yer ain special ingin."

"Was it grown organically?" Harry asked. Mario threw up his arms,

"Organic, shmorganic," he said. "It came wi' it's ain-a medical certificate," he said."

"Right, Mario," Harry said, "Ah'll get away hame wi' these before they get cauld."

"Aye, you-a dae that," Mario said.

Harry walked away then, turning at the door, called over to Mario. "We've got a wee cat in oor close. Ah think Ah'll gie it a wee treat," he said, "Gimme a single fish."

" You no' want a married wan?" Mario said facetiously

"Less o' the levity, Mario," Harry said.

"Whit's this-a levity mean?" Mario said.

"Ye know whit levity means," Harry said.

"Aw, *levity*," Mario cried, always trying to prove his command of the English language. "That's the wee-a Jewish tailor in Bain-Steet, eh?"

Harry smiled and nodded. "Right," he said, "Noo, whit aboot that fish?"

"Wan-a fish for the cat in the close, that's-a nice." Mario said. "Noo, jist a fish, eh? Ye don't-a want it tae come frae any special ocean naw?"

"Ah, noo ye're bein' facetious, Mario," Harry said."

"Ah canny be-a that," Mario said.

"How no'?"

"Ah don't-a know whit it-a means. Right," he went on,

slapping a fish on the paper, "wan-a fish, nae strings attached."

"Jist wan thing, Mario," Harry said.

"Whit's-a that," Mario aske suspicious;ly.

"Have ye got a fish called Wanda?"

Mario threw up his arms again and gazed towards heaven. "Mama Mia!" he cried.

Harry burst out laughing and Mario joined in.

Chortling loudly Mario slapped Harry on the back. "Ye're an awful man, Harry," he laughed. "Be fussy – be fussy wi' wee McNab. Ah've-a heard a' aboot him. If he he comes here Ah'll smother his chips wi' salt.".

"Don't forget the ascetic acid." Harry laughed.

"For him Ah'll make it battery acid," Mario chuckled.

"Thanks Mario," Harry said. "Ye don't mind the bit o' fun, dae ye?" _

Mario chuckled. "Ah enjoy it," he said,"Ah know you-a try for to rile me for a wee laugh. Ah don't-a mind. But wan thing, Harry . . ."

"Whit's that?" Harry asked.

"Keep yer mooth-a shut when the shoap's-a busy, eh?"

Harry laughed and waved as he made his exit with Mario's voice in his ears..

"Tell-a wee Sadie for to stick tae her-a guns, Harry," Mario called, "remember the-a Alamo."

★　★　★

Harry was still chuckling as he entered the house. Sadie was sitting by the fire looking through an old photo album. She put the album aside and joined Harry at the table. She had the tea prepared and poured out two cupfuls. The bread was already buttered and they both ate hungrily.

"Oh, ye canny beat a nice fish supper," Sadie said, wiping her mouth witha serviette."

"Ah had Mario goin' for minute," Harry said. "He says ye've tae stick tae yer guns,"

"Aye, well ye know whit they say in the pictures," Sadie said.

"Whit's that?" Harry asked.

"Ye canny fight City Hall," Sadie said.

"We're no' oot yet," Harry said.

"Ah wish Ah had your confidence," Sadie said, "but Ah canny see any wey oot o' this awful situation."

Sadie tidied up and flopped back on to the couch. Harry poured himself a dram and offered one to Sadie who shook her head. He joined her on the couch. The fire was still faming merrily. Sadie began, once more flicking through the photo album with Harry taking in the pages as they turned.

"Aw, mind that?" Sadie said joyfully, nostalgia flooding over her. "Norman and Maggie at Rothesay! Mind it poured when we waited for the boat at Wemyss Bay and Maggie fell in a puddle – her in her new froak, tae?"

Harry nodded and his mind went back. "Aye, hen, Ah mind o' that," he said quietly.

"Oh, an' look – oor Peggy's weddin' " Sadie enthused, "Ah was her best maid an the neighbours showered me wi' confetti when Ah went oot the close – aw, remember that?"

Harry looked at the photograph. "Aye, ye looked lovely, hen," he said. He knew how going through this album was tearing at Sadie's heart

"An' look," Sadie said pointing to a picture, "There's Auld Mrs McTavish. Gone noo like so many others," she said sadly, "O, an' look – Wee Effie Sweeney – she went tae America wi' her Yankee boyfriend – Wee Effie," There was genuine fondness in Sadie's shaking voice.

"Aye, and a' you lassies were jealous," Harry laughed.

"We were not," Sadie said, poking him the ribs with her elbow. "Oh, and look – oor Maggie on her First Holy Communion day – like a wee bride, she was. Ah remember Ah got a Provident cheque and got her wee white dress in Margaret Forrester's, in London Road. Aw, she was a wee picture – oh, an' there's ma Mammy at Millport – at the *Crocodile Rock* – Ah was away on a hired bike that day."

Sadie pressed the photo tightly to her breast.

"Whit's this wan, the Brigton Ladies Choir?" Harry said, pointing to a group photograph.

"That's a photy of oor neighbous – everybody up this close. Remember, it was a clabber roon the back when Mrs McDonald got word that her son was safe and well efter he had been posted missin' in Vietnam – mind her boy, Wullie, who had emigrated tae Australia and jined the army?"

"Aye, Ah dae, noo," Harry said.

"Aw look at them – the hale close – Pinky Morris – auld Mrs Templeton, the crabitt auld midden. She used tae complain that Norman was makin' too much noise in the close wi' his roller skates – Minnie Magee, prim an' proper wi' her nice froak – Aw, Harry. Sadie buried her head in her husband's chest.

"There, there," Harry said, pecking her cheek affectionately.

"This is oor last night in oor hoose," Sadie sobbed. "Oor weddin' anniversary – whit a present! And we hivnae even heard frae Norman or Maggie."

"Probably the postman thinks *everybody's* away frae the buildin'," Harry said.

"We seem tae still get oor electricty bill an' that," Sadie said.

"Bills have a wey o' always gettin' through, Sadie," Harry said.

"It's no' fair, Harry," Sadie sobbed, "a' this turmoil jist tae make room for a bowlin' alley or somethin'. It's jist greed – the whole world is ruled by greed, so it is. We've tae gie up oor hoose – oor life jist tae make somebody richer – it's no' fair."

Harry put an arm around Sadie's shoulders and gave her an affectionate squeeze. "Aye, people don't count, hen," he said, "But we *did* have it, hen – a' thae years – we did have it and that's somethin' tae be thankful for."

"Aye, Ah suppose so," Sadie said unconvincingly.

"Maybe we'll get a wee miracle," Harry said.

"It'll need tae be a big wan," Sadie said, adding," Miracles don't happen these days anywey."

"Ah, widnae say that," Harry said.

"Tell me wan miracle you've heard of recently?" Sadie asked.

"Partick Thistle won last week," Harry said with a twinkle.

"Och, you," Sadie said, poking him on the ribs.

Both laughed loudly. A sudden rapping at the door made Sadie jump.

"Who could that be?" she gasped.

"Who knows," Harry said. They stood under the skylight.

"Who's that?" Sadie called.

"*Evening Times,*" a man voice replied.

"We get it," Harry said.

"No, we're frae the *Evening Times*," the voice said. "Is that Mr McPhatter?"

"Aye, it is," Harry replied.

"Can we have a word wi' you?" The man said.

Harry looked at Sadie questioningly. Sadie nodded.

"Whit have we got tae lose?" she said.

"Aye. a' right," Harry said opening the door.

Two men squeezed in through the narrow opening of the door. "Hi, Ah'm Joe McEwan," the younger man said. "I'm a reporter in the *Times* and this is Sam Fitzgibbons," he said, pointing to his colleague who carried a metal, silver-coloured camera case.

"Sit doon, son," Sadie said.

Joe McEwan pulled a notebook from his pocket while Sam knelt on the floor and took his camera from the case.

"Ah believe you are the last two tenants up this building and are holding out, refusin' to go – that right?"

"That's right," Sadie said, "it's oor Ruby Weddin' anniversary and we're gettin' evicted the morra."

"Why will you no' go?" Joe said, licking his pencil and jotting something down.

"'Cos they hivnae oaffered us a suitable place," Sadie said

"What do you think of Mr Hector McNab?" the reporter asked, pencil poised.

"Well," Sadie said, "lct's put it this wey. If he was mentioned in the Bible he'd be the Bad Samaritan."

Joe McEwan smiled. "D'ye mind if Sam takes yer picture?" he asked.

"Is this gonny be in the paper?" Sadie asked a little nervously

"It'll be in tomorrow's edition" Joe said.

Sadie was shaking with excitement. Her picture in the paper! The only time she thought her picture in the paper would be in the obituary column of the *Scottish Catholic Observer*.

"Would youse try an place ma photy next tae wan o' George Clooney?" she said.

Joe shook his head. "Sorry", he said, "you're a news story. George Clooney would be on our television pages."

"That's a'right," said Sadie, "We have an affinity wi' him. We wull soon be steyin' in a television boax."

"If I can get you on the same page as George Clooney, I will, Mrs McPhatter," Joe smiled.

"Ye can call me Whitney," Sadie said.

"Yer name's Sadie," Harry cried.

"Only because ma Maw wis tone deef," Sadie said.

"We think it's a diabolical liberty that you should be getting evicted after spending your entire life in this close," Joe said sympathetically.

"Well, that's no' entirely true," Sadie said. "A loat o' the time we steyed in the hoose."

Joe and Sam's eyes met and they smiled.

"But the building must be condemned for a reason." Joe said.

"It's us that's condemned," Harry said. "There's nothin' wrang wi' the buildin'. It's like a ship – sturdy an' solid. If a ship's condemned ye see the rats leavin' by the battalion. Ye've heard the sayin' *Like rats leavin' a sinkin' ship. Oor* buildin' is *nut* sinkin'. They jist want the space – for some commercial, greedy purpose." Harry's blood pressure was rising rapidly. "In fact it's the other wey aboot," he went on, "The rats are movin' in. Ah saw a crowd o' them comin' up the close just the other day. Noo that is nut cognizant wi' a condemned buildin'."

Joe smiled.

"Ah've never even had ma name is the papers before," Sadie said.

"Well, it'll be in tomorrow, " Joe said. "You've got some guts fightin' for your principles. It's meeting folk like you that makes me glad to be a reporter."

"Would you like a wee hauf?" Harry asked.

"No' while workin'," Joe said.

"You must be a new breed o' reporter," Harry said.

"Have ye been a reporter long, son?" Sadie asked.

"I've been in the Press for fifteen years," Joe McEwan said proudly.

"Aw, it must be great tae get oot or a breath o' fresh air," Sadie said. "Ye're obviously no' claustrophobic."

Joe and Sam burst out laughing. "What about yer family?" Joe asked.

"Well, ma son, Norman, vanished in Canada. We checked wi'

the Canadian polis."

"And what did they say?" Joe asked, jotting in his notebook.

"The said oor Norman was a felony."

"A felony?" Joe's brows shot up.

"Aye, a fel-ony-body knows," Sadie laughed.

"So, you're just waitin' for the bulldozers, then?" Joe said.

"That's it. We just had a fish supper, even the condemned man and wumman is entitled tae a last meal, eh?" said Harry.

"You sound pretty cheery, if ye don't mind me sayin' so Mr McPhatter."

"There's a good reason for that son," Harry said.

"Oh, and what's that, Mr McPhatter," Joe asked.

"Ah'm drunk," Harry said.

"Well, you've every right to be," Joe said.

Sam stood up camera in hand.

"Mind if Ah flash," Mrs McPhatter?" he said.

"If that's whit turns ye on, son," Sadie chuckled."

Sam blushed. "Ah mean take yer picture" he said, "some people don't like the flash."

"Go ahead, son," Sadie said.

"Would ye mind staunin' at the door haudin' a rollin' pin wi' yer erms folded defiantly?" Sam said.

"Ye want me tae put on ma *Xena*, the Warrior Princess costume? Sadie said.

Sam's eyes lit up. "Have ye got wan?" he cried.

Harry laughed. "A' she needs is her pinny and wi' her rollin' pin, look out."

Sam looked disappointed. He flashed off a couple of shots.

"Well, we'll be goin'," Joe said. "Good luck the morra."

"Wull youse be here?" Sadie asked.

"We wouldn't miss it for the world," Joe said.

"Sure ye don't want a wee hauf, son?" Harry called.

"No, thanks," Joe said.

"Ach, they don't make them like James Cagney noo adays," he grumbled .

"Mair like Clark Kent," Sadie volunteered.

Four

❧ ❧ ❧

HARRY AND SADIE PUSHED THE COUCH BACK OVER TO obstruct the door. Harry poured another drink.

"Well," He said, "If Clark Kent disnae want a drink Ah dae." He offered Sadie a glass which she refused.

She drew the curtain aside and gazed out into the quiet street. Turning quickly and puting her hand to her mouth she asked frowning, "They widnae pull the buildin' doon wi' us still in it, would they?"

"Who knows whit that wee skelf would dae," Harry said, sipping his drink.

A loud knock on the door made Sadie turn quickly.

"Who could that be?" she said, a tremble in her voice. "It widnae be them already, would it?"

Harry took a quick glance out of the window. "Naw, there's nae bulldozers there," he said. He pulled the couch away from the door.

"Who is it?" Sadie called, wringing her hands nervously.

"It's me," a man's voice said.

"Who's me?" Harry called.

"The one who brings comfort," a reverent voice said.

"Aw, it's a' right, Sadie, it's big Malky frae the off-licence," Harry said, relief in his voice.

They pulled the couch away and Father Brendan McFungus walked in.

"Ah – er – thought you were Big Malky frae the off-licence bringin' me comfort," Harry said, a little embarrassed.

"Ah bring youse spiritual comfort," Father said.

"When ye said ye were bringin' us comfort Ah thought ye meant *Southern Comfort*," Harry said.

"Come in, come in, Father," Sadie said, gesturing towards the couch."It's funny, intit, we were just talkin' aboot you a wee while ago."

"We're a' worried, Father, " Harry said, "Life has just crumbled a' roon' aboot us," Harry sighed.

"Now, son, nane o' that thinkin'," the priest said, "Everying is cut oot for ye in this life – except maybe that suit ye're wearin'. That's obviously been cut oot for somebody else – Charlie Chaplin, maybe."

Sadie sighed. Father McFungus hadn't mellowed with age. He was as blunt as ever.

"Aye, it's funny," Harry said, "Jist talkin' aboot ye . . ."

"Hauf the parish are daein' that," Father McFungus said. "Ah just thought Ah'd pey youse a wee visit. Ah've heard o' the terrible hole ye're in."

"Ah beg your pardon, Father," Sadie said from her high horse, "this maybe a hole tae you but it's oor hoose – oor *Home* tae us."

"Naw, naw, Ah meant yer problem," the priest said.

"Aye, ye spend yer hale life in a place, got a' its memories and then ye're chucked oot like an auld rag."

"We'll no' talk aboot Harry's suit again," the Father said.

"It's no' fair, Father," Harry said.

"No' till July, son," the priest replied, meaning the Glasgow Fair when the annual summer holiday comes round.

"Ye hivnae chinged, Father, " Sadie said.

"Aulder, hen," the priest said, "time catches up wi' ye before ye know it. Ah was shocked wan day when Ah looked in the mirror and saw that long. grey hair."

"A' auld men grow grey hair," Harry said.

"No' oan their tongue, the don't," the priest said.

"Ye hivnae chinged much, Father, efter a' these years," Sadie said.

"Aye, well, " the priest took a deep sigh, "we are all in God's hands. We are part of the divine plan. Some people are destined tae chinge others no'.Some people look their age, others not."

"Well, you hivnae chinged, that's for sure," Sadie repeated.

"Ah'm thankful for that," the priest said. "Tae some people the shock of suddenly gettin' auld can kill them. Look at Auld Charlie McPhee. Wan minute he was a young man, the next he was an auld man. Wan look at hisel' in the mirror and he drapped deid."

"The shock of suddenly turnin' intae an auld man was too much for him?" Sadie asked, shaking her head.

"Naw, the shock o' turnin' intae an auld wumman," Father said.

"Was it somethin' in his make up?" Harry asked.

"He didnae wear any," the priest said, "At least no' then. When he went tae a cosmetic surgeon, that plastic surgeon took forty years aff him,"

"Whit did the doactor dae?" Harry asked.

"He gave him the face of Clark Gable."

"Lucky Charlie McPhee," Sadie said.

"No' really, he was still a wumman," the priest said.

"Ah think you're pullin' ma leg, Father," Sadie said.

"Ah'm tryin' tae cheer ye up," the priest said, standing up and letting his eyes sweep around the room.

"A lovely wee hoose," he said. "But Ah don't see any holy pictures on yer wa' – pictures o' saints an' that. Every Catholic home should have holy pictures on the wa'. Nut only do youse nut have a picture of St Francis of Assisi, youse don't even have wan o' Jock Stein, of Parkheid."

"We did have a picture of St Francis up on that wa'," Sadie said.

"A wonderful saint!" Father McFungus said, "He is the patron saint of animals. He loved all animals – all creatures great and small. Whit happend tae his picture?"

"We had tae take it doon," Sadie said.

"Oh, and why was that?" the priest asked.

"It frightened the cat," Harry said.

"Whit aboot yer family, yer weans?" Father asked.

"Naw, it didnae frighten them," Sadie said.

"Ah meant where are they in yer hour of need?"

"They left here wan day tae go tae Rothesay and got on the wrang boat and ended up in Canada," Sadie said sadly.

"That's life intit?" the priest said, "the fledglings fly frae the nest the minute they get their wings."

"Aye, right enough," Harry said "Ma Maw was devasted when Ah left the hoose."

"Whit age were ye?" Father asked.

"Four," Harry said.

"Ah can understaun' her concern," the priest said.

"This is oor Ruby Weddin' anniversary, Father, " Sadie piped up.

"Aye, Ah remember the day you came and asked me tae mairry you," Father said. "It was the wan day Ah was gled Ah was a priest. No' only was it impossible for me tae mairry ye, Ah was surprised he wanted ta."

"Aw, ye hivnae chinged, Father," Sadie said, "ye're still a wag,"

"Ah've never set foot in that country," the priest said.

"Whit country?" Sadie said, raising her brows, "Ah jist said ye were still a wag."

"Oh, Ah thought ye said a wog," Father McFungus said with a chuckle..

"Ah thought ye'd have been promoted by this time, Father," Harry said. "Ah mean, auld Father McShane was made a canon."

"Aye, well he was fond o' a barrel," Father McFungus said.

"Whit aboot yersel', Father? Nae sign o' promotion?" Sadie asked.

"Aye well," Father McFungus said, almost in a whisper, "an' Ah widnae want this tae get around – no yet," he put his finger to his lips. "There's a strong possibility that Ah might be becomin' a Monsignor,"

"Ye're becomin' a *Frenchman!*" Sadie cried in surprise.

"Don't be daft, Sadie," Harry rebuked his wife, "Er – monsignor – means *My auld pensioner* – French – Mon – means My and Signor – means senior – senior citizen, get it?"

Father McFungis said, "Ah can see you're a university graduate, Mr McPhatter,"

Harry missed his sarcasm. "Jist call me John," he said.

"Yer name's Harry," Sadie snapped.

"If you can be Whitney, Ah can be John, efter John Wayne, ma favourite," Harry said.

"Are ye retired, Harry," the priest asked.

"Ah am," Harry said, "but Ah've been attendin' night school and learnin' metalwork. Ah love workin' in bronze!"

"A bit hoat, is it no'?" Father said. "Ye'd be better workin' in a vest."

"Were you always a priest, Father?" Sadie asked.

"Naw, Ah was a wean wance," Father McFungus said.

"Ah meant did ye go straight intae the seminary straight frae school?" Sadie said.

"Ah had a vocation," Father said, "Ah liked the uniform – Ah hated hivin' tae wear a tie. Ah liked the idea o' a backward coaller."

"Did ye never work, then?" Harry asked.

"Ah did for a while.," he said, "Ah always had this thing aboot God's poor creatures. Ah loved animals – just like Saint Francis. So, Ah knew Ah'd have tae get a joab workin' wi' animals and Ah did."

"Ye became a vet, then?" Sadie said.

"Naw, a butcher," Father said

Sadie wished she hadn't asked him.

"Then, in 1942. Ah got the call," he went on.

"Aye, there was a loat of it goin' aboot then. Ah got the flu." Sadie said.

"God works in mysterious ways," Father McFungus went on. "There's only wan way to Paradise."

"A number nine caur," Harry said quickly.

"No' Celtic Park, Paradise," Father said. "Ah mean *the* Paradise. That is oor purpose on earth – to live a good life with Heaven as oor goal. Ah thought ma particular wey was to become a priest so Ah stopped studyin' the hoarses and started studyin theology."

"That him that was in *Kojak*?" Sadie said. "His name was Theo somethin'."

"His name wisnae Ology, Sadie," Harry snapped. "Naebody is called Ology. His name was Telly – called efter his profession."

Father McFungus cleared his throat. "Never be complacent, though. Ye can just never be sure that you'll get there and even if ye dae, be sure o' steyin' there. Ah mean look at poor Lazarus. Wan minute he's walkin' doon the golden mile in heaven. Suddenly he finds himsel' a' swathed in bandages and bein' telt tae get up an' come oot his grave. No' only is he plucked from

106

the glory of heaven, his eternal reward. He's no' even wearin' a decent suit."

"An' we're worried because we're gettin' slung oot just oor hoose," Sadie said.

"There's a lesson tae be learned there," Harry said.

"Whit's that?" Sadie asked.

"When Ah snuff it bury me in ma crombie coat."

"How? dae ye think *you* might get whipped oot o' heaven and sent back doon here tae earth?" Sadie said.

"Ah'm takin' nae chances," Harry said. "If it could happen tae Lazarus, it could happen tae me. Ah refuse point blank tae walk doon the street in a shroud."

"The situation will never arrive, Harry," Sadie said. "For a start ye'll never see heaven and if ye are sent back, ye'd better jist get buried in yer biler suit. It's harder diggin' yer wey up than comin' doon on a parachute."

"Nae fightin'," the priest said.

"Ah'm only kiddin', Father," Sadie said. "Harry will see heaven. He's been a good man tae me. But Ah don't want him tae be complacent, the Devil's wily."

"Quite right tae be careful," the priest said.

"Ah'm sure Hector McNab is wan o' his disciples," Sadie said.

"Aye, it's a shame ye've tae leave this lovely wee hoose. Is yer wallpaper made o' recycled paper?" Father said, looking round the house.

"Whit makes she say that, Father?" Sadie asked.

"It's covered in tyre marks," the priest said.

"Oh, that's just Harry on his mountain bike," Sadie said. "Practising runnin' up and doon the wa'."

"Did he become proficient?" the priest asked.

"Oh, naw, he steyed a Catholic, Father," Sadie said.

"Y'know, Father, Ah was very nearly a man o' the cloth masel' wance," Harry said.

"Ye were thinkin' aboot becomin' a priest, eh?" the priest said.

"Na, an apprentice tailor," Harry said. "Although ma teacher at school suggested Ah should become a lifeguard."

"Who wants tae be a bar o' soap?" Sadie said.

"Ah meant . . ."

"Only kiddin', Harry," Sadie said. "But Ah dae think you might've been a good tailor, staunin' there cuttin' the cloth."

"Ah think Ah would've been good at cuttin'," Harry said.

"Well, ye're were always hauf cut for *a start*," Sadie said.

Father McFungus stood up. "Aye, well," he said, "when Ah heard youse two were in this buildin' haudin' oot, Ah thought Ah'd come up and see if there was anythin' Ah could dae tae help?"

"Well, we want tae leave the hoose in a presentable state," Harry said, "You could waash the windaes."

"*Harry!*" Sadie rebuked.

"Just the inside," Harry said in defence.

"A prayer would help." Father said, "Why don't ye have a word wi' that great miracle worker, St Francis?" he added

"It's us we're worried aboot, no' the cat," Harry said.

"He listens to all prayers," Father McFungus said.

"Ah don't think he'll listen tae anythin' Ah've got tae say," Harry said.

"And why not?" Father said, narrowing his eyes.

"Ah wance had oor pet rottweiler spayed."

"But that's quite in order," the priest said.

"No' when it's a boy dug, it's no'."

"It was a mistake, obviously," the priest said.

"It was. Faher, we'd just the dug – fully grown it was – a week, when Ah took it tae the vet." Harry sounded contrite.

"Ah'll be the vet was surprised," Father said.

"No' as surprised as the dug was," Harry said.

"Well, Ah don't think St Francis would fa' oot wi' ye for a genuine mistake like that," Father McFungus said.

"The dug did," Harry said.

"It's understandable," Father said.

"He used tae come intae the room every moarnin', jump intae bed and lick and play wi' ma big toe," Harry said.

"He stopped jumpin intae yer bed and playin' wi' yer big toe?" Father asked.

"He did," Harry said, "he took ma toe doon tae his ain bed."

"Don't you believe him, Father," Sadie said.

Ah thought he was pullin' ma leg," the priest said.

"Too true," Sadie said. "It was ootside it used tae play wi' it."

"So, when dae youse expect for to be evicted?" Father McFungus asked with some pity.

"The morra," Sadie said. "We've naewhere tae go."

"Never mind, the priest said, "your home is in heaven."

"Some good that is when we're still doon here," Sadie said.

"Ah was thinkin' in gettin' a big Hitachi boax," Harry said.

"Ah know a bloke who moved intae a big Hitachi boax," he priest said.

"Whit happened?" Sadie asked, curiously

"He ended up goin' tae see a psychiatrist aboot his dreams," the priest said.

"Whit aboot his dreams?" Sadie getting more curious.

"He couldnae understaun' them," Father said.

"How no'?" Sadie asked.

"They were a' in Japanese," the priest said, a naughty glint in his eye.

"Aw, away wi' ye, ye're pullin' ma leg," Sadie laughed.

"Ah'm just tryin' tae relieve the tension, Sadie," Father said."Wi' God's help everythin' wull turn oot a'right, you'll see,"

"Thanks, Father," Sadie said, meaning it with all her heart.

"Aw, Father," Harry cried, "Ah never even oaffered ye a wee refreshment,"

"Ah know," the priest said, "Well, Ah'd better go and see tae ma flock."

"Oh, are ye takin' up sheep farmin', Father?" Harry said.

"Ah'm goin' ta see wan o' ma parishioners who was recently bereaved."

"Oh, who wis that, Father?" Sadie asked.

"Poor Mrs Magee. Her husband, Horace departed," the priest said. "Ah only hope Ah find her standin' up and facin' her bereavement."

"Ah just hope ye find her staunin' up," Harry said.

"*Harry!*" Sadie snapped.

Father McFungus turned at the door, "May the Lord deliver you," he said.

"Well if he disnae, Pickfords will," Sadie replied.

Father Fungus took his leave.

"Well, Sadie said, "that was a surprise – Father McFungus."

"He looks the same," Harry said.

"Aye, well at least we know we've got *his* prayers," Sadie said.

"Ah'd rather have his spare room," Harry said. "D'ye think Mrs O'Brien's still wi' him?"

Sadie shook her head. "Ah would think she'd be aboot a hunner year auld by noo," Sadie said.

"It's no impossible," Harry said. "Ah mean, look at the auld Queen Mother for a start. And don't forget Irvin' Berlin lived till he was a hunner and wan and that great Cockney actress Kathleen Harrison was a hundred an' three when she died. Nuthin's impossible, hen!"

"Ah but they two lived cosseted lives. Ah mean the auld Queen Mother had lackeys tae run efter her and Irvin Berlin spent his life sittin' doon at a pianna. Ah mean they had easy lives. Mrs O'Brien would be run aff her feet in that big hoose, people at the door a' the time. Naw, Ah think she's gone up there and Father McFungus would've oaffered us his spare room if he had wan." Sadie sounded as though she talked with authority.

* * *

Sadie and Harry passed the night watching television. Tomorrow was another day. Sadie tried to put the thought out of her mind but now and again Harry would hear a quiet sob. Before retiring to bed they piled up furniture at the door and snibbed the window.

"Right," Sadie said, "they'll have tae drag us oot."

She put her head on the pillow and thought of Norman and Maggie. Harry snored The sound of a heavy truck rumbling down the street made Sadie jump. She blinked her eyes as the morning sunshine streamed through the window, She nudged Harry, still snoring, in the ribs.

"Harry – Harry," she whispered." Harry, waken up."

Harry grumbled, rubbed his eyes and then realised the urgency in Sadie's voice. He sat bolt upright.

"Whit is it – ? Whits is it – ?" he yelled.

"Listen," Sadie said, "the bulldozers."

But all was quiet now. To pacify Sadie, Harry got up and pulled back the curtain of the window. Only a stray cat could be seen crossing the street, He looked at the clock – seven o'clock. Harry climbed back into bed.

"Go to sleep, hen. It's your imagination." Harry was sound within a minute.

Five

✠ ✠ ✠

"SIR MURDO MCWHACHLE WULL SEE YOU NOW."

Hector McNab followed the clerk into the panelled office of Sir Murdo McWhachle, the city's housing supremo. Sir Murdo, a tall, thin man with a Hitler moustache stood, his back to the door, gazing out of the large window.

Hector stood, uncomfortably shuffling his feet, in front of the huge mahogany desk waiting for his master to acknowledge his presence. Hector gave a quiet cough. Sir Murdo turned and eyed the little man before him.

"So, McNab, " he said gruffly, " what's holding up the demolishing of this building in Glenvernon Street?"

"Er – well – er –" Hector stammered, "it – er –"

"We're behind schedule," Sir Murdo snapped. "That building has to come doo – er – down or Cochrane, Cochrane and McSmith will withdraw their offer – their *very generous* offer, to build their millennium tower

"Ah – er – I thought they were building a bowling alley?" Hector said.

"That was the original idea," Sir Murdo said, "but Mr McSmith's wife ran away wi' a bowling alley manager."

"And so he canny bear tae think of him doin' anythin' to promote that game – it's too painful, that it?" Hector asked.

"No, no, he wants for to build a tower in celebration," Sir Murdo said.

"Whit kind o' tower?" Hector asked, raising his eyebrows.

"You know – like the CN Tower, in Toronto, or the Centre Point Tower, in Sydney. It would be a wonderful landmark for our city," Sir Murdo said with obvious enthusiasim.

"We've got enough towers in the city," Hector said, "wi' a' they high flats. They are *not* popular."

"We high heid yins must make decisions that are not popular," Sir Murdo said, forgetting his acquired patois.

"Whit good's a tower gonny be?" Hector asked.

"We'll have a restaurant and bar at the very top that goes roon' and roon' It will bring to life the lyrics of that famous song, "whit's the maitter wi' Glesca 'cos it's goin' roon an' roon".

"A' ye need for Glesca tae go roon and roon is a couple whiskies – no' a bloody big tower," Hector said, finding courage.

"Towers are wonderful things," Sir Murdo enthused, "Look at the Blackpool Tower, the Eiffel Tower, in Paris – both wonderful tourist attractions. So, whit's the big hold up?"

"It's a couple called the McPhatters," Hector said. " They jist don't want to move and they've turned doon – er – down every offer Ah've made them."

"Well, make them an offer they can't refuse," Sir Murdo said.

"Dae ye think the Queen would consider rentin' oot Windsor Castle?" Hector said couragously, if not facetiously

"Come, come, now," Sir Murdo said. "It just takes a liile tact when dealing with these people. You have to learn how to handle the peasants, McNab," Sir Murdo said.

"You hivnae met Sadie McPhatter," Hector said.

"You've heard the famous expression uttered by Marie Antoinette, *Let them eat cake*. You know who she was, don't you?"

"A Paris Bun?" Hector said.

"She was Queen of France. She lost her head."

"And so will Ah if Ah forcefully evict this dynamic duo."

"When are you planning to make your move?" Sir Murdo asked.

"This efter – er – afternoon," Hector said,

"I shall come with you," Sir Murdo said, his chest swelling, "Ah know how to handle these people."

"Well, if you've got a suit of armour, wear it," Hector said.

"Anything else?" Sir Murdo said.

"Well, if you've got a spare machine gun!"

"Don't you worry about a thing. I'm an expert at throwing people out of their homes. The McPhatters are really squatting!" Sir Murdo declared.

"Well, there's nae need for it," Hector said "they've still got their chairs an' that."

"No, I meant they're there illegally," Sir Murdo said, giving Hector a puzzled look.

"Ah really appreciate ye takin' things in hand, Sir Murdo," Hector grovelled.

"Think nothing of it m'boy," Sir Murdo said. "I have found myself in the most difficult positions. You must talk to these people with compassion in you voice, you see, I remember a similar situation where a travelling family had taken over a bungalow in the south side while the owner was on holiday. They would not budge. I felt sorry for them, all those wee faces pressed against the window. There were ten children in the family, the mother, the father and the dog. 'You will have to leave,' I told them in my most compassionate tone."

"And what did they say?" Hector asked.

"Their little five-year-old daughter came to the door. My heart went out to her. She stood there, her wee frock tattered and torn. Her snotty wee nose and grubby face. A sad sight, it was."

"What did she say?" Hector asked again.

"She said, 'Shut yer bloody face, you,' and slammed the door."

"Whit did ye dae," Hector asked, forgetting his posh accent.

"I blew the hoose up," Sir Murdo said."Ah mean one cannot have the peasants dictating to one, can one?"

Hector shrugged. Sir Murdo took his bowler hat and umbrella from the stand, opened the door wide and beckoned to Hector. "Right," he said, " let's get this over with."

They walked into the bright sunlight of George Street and turned up towards George Square. Sir Murdo walked briskly an Hector had a job keeping up with him.

"We have to be careful we do not rile the public in this matter," Sir Murdo said. "At the same time they like to see that their representatives are strong willed. I'd like to take a lead here."

"Ah think you'd be better goin' up tae the toilets in Queen Street Station," Hector said, pointing with his thumb in the general direction.

114

"What's that got to do with me wanting to take a lead here?" Sir Murdo asked.

"Oh, Ah thought ye said ye wanted to take a leak," Hector said.

Murdo made no reply but was rapidly coming to the conclusion that Hector needed all the *assistance he could get.*

The cry of a newspaper vendor made them stop in their track.

"*Evening Times, Evening Times,*" was the cry, "Globble – bliggle hooseo ootoo," the vendor cried in what was obviously Swahili.

Sir Murdo paid the man and, with Hector peering over his shoulder, swept his eyes over the front page.

Fighting Sadie ready for Battle, screamed the headlines with a picture of Sadie standing with a defiant look on her face, and holding her rolling pin.

"She looks quite formidable," Sir Murdo said, gulping.

"She is," Hector emphasised.

"Right, let's go then," Sir Murdo said.

* * *

Sadie poured the tea and kept glancing towards the window fearful of catching sight of a bulldozer. Her ears, too, were fine tuned. All was quiet outside. The sudden loud knocking on the door made her jump.

"That's *him,* Ah'll bet it is," she cried.

"We'll see, Harry said, giving the barricade a good final shove against the door. Sadie had already packed two suitcases with their clothes and while determined not to leave meekly, knew she was facing the inevitable.

The knocking the the door was persistant.

"Who is it?" Sadie called.

"Open the door and see," a man's voice replied.

Sadie and Harry looked at each other.

"*Norman!*" they cried together.

Quickly they began to dismantle their fortress and throw the door wide open. Norman McPhatter stood on the doorstep resplendent in the scarlet uniform of the Royal Canadian Mounted Police.

Norman swept his mother into his arms and smothered her with kisses. Harry pumped his son's hand and steered him through the door and into the room. Once safely inside Harry shoved his barriacde back and with a final shove, made sure it was secure.

"Geez!" Norman exclaimed, "this puts me in mind o' Fort Matilda when the Algonquins attacked."

"Aw, son, it's lovely for tae see ye hame efter a' these years. Whit happened," Sadie said, her voice shaking.

"Well Maw," Norman began, "Maggie an' me went doon tae get the ferry tae Rothesay that day. We got on the boat and off it went. Ah thought the trip would tak a couple o' 'oors at the maist but when we went intae oor second day Ah began tae wonder. Then we saw a polar bear floatin' by oon an iceberg an' Ah turned tae Maggie an' said, 'Ah don't think ye get polar bears near Rothesay'. And Ah was right. We arrived in Canada and that was it."

"Aw, ye're hame noo and that's a' that matters," Harry said.

"Whit did ye no' write tae us for, then?" Sadie scolded.

"We did write but we kept gettin' oor letters back sayin *Gone Away.*" Norman said.

"That's that glaiket postman," Harry said. "Ah'll bet he thought everybody up the buildin' was away."

"Ah was always suspicious of him when Ah saw his white stick," Sadie said.

"So, when did ye join the Boy Scouts, son?" Harry asked.

"This isnae a boy scouts uniform, Da'," Norman said. "This is the uniform of the Royal Canadian Mounted Polis."

"Ah, Rose Marie!" Sadie twittered.

"Ma name's Norman, Maw," Norman said.

"Ah know yer name, son, Ah had ye christened," Sadie said. "When ye said the Royal Canadian Mounted polis, Ah immediately thought of Nelson Eddy and Jeanette McDonald – they used tae communicate across the Rocky Mountains singin' *When Ah'm Callin' You...ooo...ooo*," Sadie's tonsils were in fine tune.

"We don't dae that noo, Maw," Norman said. "We've got mobile phones noo."

"Ach it's no' the same, is it!" Sadie said.

Norman nodded to the suitcases sitting on the middle of the floor. "Are youse goin' somewhere?" he asked.

"We're gettin' thrown oot, son, "Sadie said, dabbing the corner of her eye.

"And is that the reason for the Alamo there," Norman said, nodding towards the barricaded door."

"Aye, son, Harry said, there's a wee scunner called McNab oot tae chuck us intae the street."

"No' oot *Oor Hoose* where Ah growed up?" Norman said in disbelief. For this was the only house Norman ever knew in the city of his birth. His boyhood memories were all here packed within' these walls. He couldn't believe it was all to go.

"They want tae demolish the buildin', son," Sadie said, "They say it's condemned."

"It looks a' right tae me," Norman said.

"Wi' your eyes nuthin' looks a'right tae you," Harry said."Remember ye used tae wear jeely-jaur specs when ye were a wee boy?"

"Aye. they were really uncomfortable, and heavy," Norman said."Youse should really have taken oot the strawberry jam first."

"Ye were seein' life through rose-coloured specs, son, eh?" Harry laughed.

"A' them happy memories still in yer heid, son, eh?" Sadie said.

"They are inedibly cherished in ma heart, Mammy," Norman said, pointing to the right ide of his chest.

"Aw, that's nice son," Sadie said.

Norman let his eyes sweep the room.

"That's the same auld couch Ah used tae play on, intit?" he said pointing.

"Naw, it's no', son," Harry said.

"Oh, did ye buy a new wan?" Norman said with disappointment.

"Naw, that's the sideboard, Norman," Harry said.

"Er – how did ye ever manage tae get intae the mounties, son?" Sadie asked.

"It was an advert in the paper, maw," Norman said. " It said the mounties were lookin' for cowboys and Ah remembered that before Ah went tae Canada and Ah was workin' here as a painter an' decorator, people whose hooses Ah'd did used tae call me a cowboy. So Ah applied."

"Whit aboot Bella, son?" Sadie asked.

"Naw, she's no' a mountie." Norman said.

"Naw, Ah meant did you an' her get merried?"

"We did, " Norman said, beaming broadly.

"And is she ower here wi' you?" Harry asked.

"Naw, Ah suppose she's away travellin' wi' her man," Norman said.

"Whit dae ye mean, 'Her Man'?", Sadie snapped. "Ah thought you said youse had got merried?"

"And so we did, Maw," Norman said, "but no' tae each other. Bella had the circus in her blood. She wanted for tae be aroon' animals a' the time. Animals were her whole life. In fact when she took ill she never went tae a doactor. She went tae a vet."

"So, whit happened between you two?" Sadie went on.

"Bella threw me up. Ah didnae mind that but Ah was hingin' ower the balcony at the time. She finally ran away wi' a elephant trainer and they baith did a double act."

"The cheek o' her!" Sadie said.

"It was a great act, mind ye," Norman said. "Bella would lie doon on her back and this big elephant would put it's big foot oan her face. "

Bella had such a nice face, tae," Sadie said.

"No' noo, she hisnae," Norman said.

"So, you're a bachelor boy then, son?" Harry said, slapping Norman on the back.

"Oh, naw, " Norman said, "Ah met a lovely Indian squaw and fell madly in love."

"A full blooded Indian squaw, eh?" Harry said, thinking of Jeanette McDonald.

"Well, no' really full-blooded," Norman said. "Her maw was Irish – so, she was really a squawleen, Ah suppose."

"How did ye meet ma daughter-in-law?" Sadie said excitedly.

"Ah was trailin' a man for a thousand miles and accidently stumbled intae that Indian camp."

"Whit horrendous thing had he done, son, that ye had ta trail him for a thousand miles?" Harry said with admiration.

118

"He had illegally shot a moose," Norman said.

"And ye trailed him for a thousand miles for *that*?" Sadie cried,"Geez, we dae that a' the time. We've got hunners o' them in this hoose and we kill them a' the time."

"Oor moose have big hoarns, Maw, and staun' aboot six feet high," Norman said.

"Geez Ah'm gled we don't have them," Sadie cried, bringing her hand to her mouth. "Think o' the size o' the holes in the wa'."

Harry and Norman glanced knowingly at each other and smiled.

"So that's where ye met ye're bride-tae-be – in that Indian camp, eh?" Harry said.

"That's right, Da' Norman said. "Ah had just arrived and bent doon tae enter her tent –"

"Teepee," Harry corrected.

"Naw, Ah'd been tae the toilet earlier," Norman said.

"They call their tents tepees, son," Harry said.

"Well, anywey," Norman went on, "Ah went in tae ask her faither if he had seen this moose-killer and was attracted tae her immediately Ah set ma eyes on her. She was skinnin' a buffalo at the time despite the protests."

"Frae her faither?" Harry asked.

"Naw, the buffalo," Norman said. "It wisnae deid at the time."

"Whit's yer squaw's name, son?" Sadie said, showing interest.

"She's called after a famous ancestor of hers," Norman said."

"Oh, whit's that, son?" Harry asked.

"Pinoccio," Norman said.

Harry and Sadie glanced at each other.

"Called efter a famous ancestor?" Sadie said.

"Aye, there's a statue in England somewhere erected tae the memory of her famous ancestor," Norman said proudly.

"It's no' Winston Churchill, is it?" Sadie asked.

Norman shook his head.

"Naw, she fell in love wi' a sea captain called John Smith but never married him."

"Aw, Ah know who you mean," Sadie cried. "It's no' Pinoccio, it's *Pocahontas*."

"Has she got a big nose son?" Harry asked.

"Naw, no' particularly," Norman said.

"Well, it's definitely no' Pinoccio," Harry said.

Sadie, wondering if she had become a grandmother unknown to her, asked, "Have ye any papooses, Norman?"

Norman nodded. Sadie clapped her hands together in joy. "Ah'm a granny, would ye believe it? Efter a' this time, Ah'm a granny."

Sadie was beside herself. "Whit is it ye've got, son?" she asked.

"Well, we've got a ginger tom and a tabby," Norman said.

"Oh!" Sadie said, her chin falling.

"Ah think yer Maw means have ye any weans?" Harry said.

Norman shook his head. "Naw," he said, "Pinoccio's kept busy wi' the ponies."

"Oh, she trains them?" Harry said with admiration.

"Naw, she bets them," Norman said

Harry and Sadie looked at each other. They didn't dare ask if he had caught the moose killer.

"Whit aboot oor Maggie?" Sadie said at last.

"Maggie was voted the best lumberjill in the business," Norman said.

"Good for Maggie!" Sadie said.

Harry nodded agreement. "It's hard work that, bein' a lumberjill."

"It is when you're the only wan in the camp," Norman said, "The men in the camp said Maggie's was the best lumber around."

"Are ye goin' back tae Canada, son?" Sadie asked, hoping for a negative reply.

Norman nodded. "Aye, Ah planned tae go back next week."

"Dae ye have tae go back so soon?" Sadie said, disappointed.

"Ah'm a mountie, Maw, Ah must get back tae duty. Ye know oor motto, *We always get oor man!*"

"Ye're no' gay, son, are ye?" Sadie said.

"Naw, Mammy, it's just oor motto," Norman said.

"Right, then, say it son – say it."

"Say whit , mammy?"

"Say ye're takin' yer Da' and me back wi' ye tae stey wi' ye and yer squaw and yer squaw's maw."

"Ah wish Ah could, Mammy, Norman said, "but it's just a wee tent," we've got. We were hopin' for somethin' bigger but the Big Chief s could only oaffer us the twenty-seventh flair."

"Ah didnae know ye could get high-rise tents, Harry said.

"They're sproutin' up everywhere, Harry," Sadie said.

"Aye, but twenty-seven storey tents, Sadie," Harry stammered, "That's ridiculous."

"It's hellish tryin' tae wallpaper them," Norman said.

"We've got the same problem here, son," Sadie said. "They're tryin' tae shove us intae anythin' and Ah'm no' hivin' it." Sadie tightened her lips.

"Good for you, Maw," Norman said."Where are ye gonny go so that Ah can write tae ye?"

"Just address yer letters tae the third Hitachi boax under the third pillar o' the Kingston Bridge," Sadie said.

Norman looked at Harry, his brows puckered.

"Don't believe yer maw," Harry said.

"Thank God for that, ye had me worried there," Norman said.

"It's the *fourth* pillar doon," Harry said.

A loud rumble from outside had Sadie hurrying over to the $ window. She pulled the curtain back a fraction.

"*Oh Harry!*" she cried, "They're here – bulldozers an' everything. There's a man there wi' his big ball and chain. Oh, Harry!"

"The swines!" Harry said, "No' only dae they come tae throw ye oot yer hoose, wan man has brought his wife alang wi' him."

"Naw, his ball an' chain are on a big swivel. Ah've seen it in the pictures. They swing it against yer hoose and it smashed everythin' tae pieces," Sadie yelled.

"They'll no' dae it while we're still in the hoose," Harry said.

"Oh, look," Sadie cried, "two men are comin' up the close."

Sadie's observation was followed by a loud rapping on the door.

"Who is it?" Harry called through the skylight.

"Ah am Sir Murdo McWhachle," a voice answered, "high heid yin of hooses."

"Whit dae ye want?" Sadie said.

"A fish supper," Sir Murdo said "but that's no' why I'm here."

"Whit'll we dae?" Sadie said, turning to Harry.

"Let him come in," Harry said, "Ah've heard o' him. "He's the man who blew up a bungalow in the soo' side when the people inside refused tae leave."

"It would've been worse if it had been a tower block," Sadie said.

"They'll no' blaw us up as long as he's in the hoose," Harry said.

Norman said nothing and stood playing with his woggle.

Harry and Sadie pulled back the furniture and Sir Murdo and a youngish man entered together.

"Hello," the youngish man said, "Ah'm Tommy Sherman, Chairman of the U.P.W.P,"

"Whit's that?" Sadie asked.

"Up The Workers Party," the man answered.

"Look here," Sir Murdo said, "youse are holding up progress. This building has got to come down to make way for a very important project."

"Who needs another bowlin' alley?" Sadie said.

"Not a bowling alley – a tower," Murdo said pompously

"Oh, that makes a big difference," Sadie said sarcastically.

"You don't have to be facetious," Sir Murdo said.

"Ah have never been that," Sadie said, "Ah've always been a Catholic."

"Who's the boy scout here?" Murdo asked, pointing to Norman.

"That is oor son, Norman, and he is *nut* a boy scout. He is a mountie in Canada," Sadie said proudly.

"Yukon?" Murdo said.

"Naw, Ah'm steyin'," Norman said.

"Ah should let you know that oor Norman is an expert in the martial arts," Harry said.

"Kung Fu?" Murdo said.

"Naw, he's had a wee drink right enough but he's sober enough," Harry said.

"Look Mr Murdo," Sadie began, "It's oor Ruby weddin' anniversary, we've been forty years in this hoose. We canny see how the buildin' can be condemned. It was the only buildin' in the street wi' a wally close. Everybody was that proud o' it. The tenants took great care o' their close. Ye could eat yer dinner aff the grun' in that close and a loat o' people did. We attracted tramps frae a' ower the place. 'Let's a' go tae the tile close for oor dinner,' they would cry."

Sir Murdo grinned broadly.

"You are not takin' this situation very seriously," Harry snapped, "Staunin' there beamin' frae coarner-tae-coarner."

"Ah am merely showin' aff my new £300 teeth," Murdo said, adding, "As am a compassionate man and as it's your fortieth anniversary Ah'll give youse forty minutes to vacate these premises."

"Oh naw ye'll no'," Tommy Sherman snapped. "Ah have here in ma haun a court injunction giving a three day reprieve of this horrendous attack on the workin' class."

"Ye canny dae that," Sir Murdo snapped.

"Ah've done it," Tommy Sherman said. "So you can just take yer bulldozers and scram,"

Murdo McWhachle's smile vanished. He turned on his heel and clambered over the barricade.

"Like General McArthur," he grunted, "I shall return – on Friday."

"Aye, well ye can huff and ye cann puff but ye'll no' blow this hoose doon." Tommy said.

"Or *up*," Harry added.

"We'll see," Murdo said.

Sir Murdo McWhachle stormed out of the close and with an authorative wave of the hand sent the bulldozers in reverse.

"Aw, thanks Mr Sherman," Sadie said, kissing his cheek. "whit happens noo?"

"Well," Tommy said, "The Scottish Parliament is on holiday just noo. But Ah will call a special emergency meetin' and see if Ah can get a law that makes it impossible for these over-inflated people wi' smiles tae chuck people like youse wi' yer ain teeth getting chucked oot just like that."

"But did Ah no' read that the Scottish Parliament is on holiday right noo?" Harry said.

"Ah'll get them back," Tommy said. and, with that, he left Sadie and Harry with a cheery wave.

"Whit dae ye think?" Sadie said to Harry.

"He means well but he hisnae got a £300 smile or a Sir before his name," Harry said, obviously not giving much hope to MSP Sherman's kind efforts.

"Don't depend on anythin' frae the Scottish Parliament," Harry said, putting his arm around Sadie's shoulder."They've got trouble wi' their ain hoose."

"So should we just gie up?" Sadie said.

"Naw, ye never know whit might turn up, hen. *never* gie up."

Sadie appreciated Harry comforting encouragement.

★　★　★

Telegrams and faxes were sent out immediately from Tommy Sherman's office to all Scottish Members to attend a special emergency meeting to discuss housing evictions. The M.P.'s, true Scots all who kept extolling the benefits of holidaying in Bonnie Scotland – it's magnificent scenery, Rob Roy, William Wallace. Of the sweet smelling heather. Of our Lochs and mountains. Of the hallowed places where our national drink was produced. Of our superb golf courses. They were summoned back to the hallowed halls of the Scottish Parliament Building in Edinburgh. And they came in their dozens, from Corfu, Majorca, Turkey, and Ibiza. Tommy, himself, so incensed at the McPhatter's treatment had cancelled his holiday in Dunoon to oversee this assembly.

They packed into the parliament, some with jet lag others just annoyed at their sunshine holiday being so rudely interrupted. Tommy stood up.

"This couple have just celebrated their Ruby Wedding and their son, a boy scout, has come over from Canada to celebrate it with them. Only to find that they are being ejected from the house that's been their home for the past forty years – and why? To make way for a tower."

A hand went up at the back and a woman member jumped up.

"Mr Presiding Officer," she called, "As I have come back here from my well-earned holiday, I wish to object. After all we only get seventeen weeks holiday without being called back like this."

"Quite right!" a voice called.

"We should be discussing a rise in our salaries – again," an angry voice bellowed. "Instead of wasting time with this drivel. If they've been in that house forty years it's forty years too long,"

"And what's your point Windy Sandman?" the Presiding Officer said.

"If we are called back from our well-earned holiday, we should be discussing something more important," Windy Sandman said."

"Like what for instance?" the Presiding Officer asked.

"Like repealling the iniquitous Clause 82," she said.

"Now you know we had a referendum on that and the people threw it out by a large majority," the Speaker said.

"And when did we start listening to the people?" Windy said.

"Ah'm ashamed of the lot of you," Tommy Sherman said. "People should come first. What do we do about this old couple and their boy scout son?"

"Let's have a vote," a voice said.

"Right," said the Presiding Officer. "All in favour of the McPhatters raise hauns". Only Tommy Sherman's hand went up.

"Right, all no' in favour?"

Every hand went up.

"I demand a re-count," Tommy Sherman cried, "we've no' to be too hasty here."

This was carried and the Speaker then turned to Windy Sandman, "Now, about your Repealing bill, Windy. Let's vote – all in favour of abolishing Clause 82 despite whit the public want, raise yer hauns."

The 'ayes' won it and Clause 82, that which allowed snogging in the back row of the pictures was abolished. When asked why she'd brought forward a crazy idea, Windy said: "Ah wanted ma name in the papers and become famous, so Ah did."

Sadie and Harry heard the news on the BBC's nine o'clock bulletin.

"Well, that's that!" Sadie said, dabbing her eye.

"Don't be so sure," Harry said.

The issue was raised in Westminster.

Should people accept houses they don't want? Should they be forced to quit their homes after a lifetime in them? Should towers be built on waste ground after happy families were evicted?

The questions caused a storm from the Labour benches and the Speaker, Betty Boothroyd, found it hard to control the angry membsrs.

So much so that she threatened to resign.

Placard waving crowds marched up and down outsde Parliament building.

God Bless the McPhatters – An Englishman's home is his Castle – even if he's a Scotsman – Down with Bureaucracy – Good old Windy Sandman – From Hot Lips Wullie.

The Post Office delivered petitions by the sackful. The Prime Minister demanded to know the state of the proposed building due to be demolished?

"What's going up in it's place?" he wanted to know.

"A monument to the millennium," he was told.

"Like what?" he asked.

"How do you feel about the dome? he was asked.

"I think Mr Hague is not a bad sort as far as Tories go," he replied.

When told a tower was to be erected near the Barras with a revolving sushi restaurant at the top he thought it was appropriate as he thought that particular dish was revolting.

It was decided that any decision on the problem was up to the Scottish Executive and a note was passed back to the Scottish First Minister advising him to be careful. This issue could cost votes.

* * *

Thursday came Sadie had exhausted her valium supply. Harry was laid back and Sadie wondered how he could be so complacent when their world was about to literally crash around them. Norman had hired a video of Rose Marie and was practising his *When I'm Calling yoo . . . ooo . . . ooo* in the bedroom. Tommy Sherman kept the family informed of his efforts on their behalf. The Members of the Scottish Parliament met that day although many were disgruntled at having to stay and work when they could be away following the sun.

One unknown member had secretly placed a tack on Tommy Sherman's chair. And Windy Sandman put forward a motion that the Scottish Parliament, as it was just a big, exclusive club anyway, should be re-titled Planet Holyrood and Arnold Schwarzenegger should change his name to Angus and open the new session. Also before them lay the motion that they should debate the abolishment of student fees. But this was put on the back burner as the McPhatter Crisis, as it was now called, took top priority.

The debate was delayed as the tea trolley came round followed by the ice-cream vendor followed by the picture postcard seller. And then, just before the Presiding Officer's gavel hit the board one of the members demanded that he be allowed to stand and sing a quick chorus of *My Way*. This was allowed and he finished to rapturous applause with cries of encore. He followed up by playing the assembly's adopted anthem, *The Donkey Serenade*, on the spoons. This once more, was followed by loud applause. The man took his bow and then went to the toilet.

Minutes after the Geggie Male Voice Choir. who had been getting a tour of the Parliament and learning the wages, perks and holidays of its members, sang a quick chorus of *Amazing Disgrace*, afterwards

It took just two minutes to despatch the McPhatter dispute in the bin.

Wee Malky Thomson on instructions from Tommy Sherman, was ordered to take the McPhatter's plight to the European Court of Human Rights. Tommy could not manage to go himself as he was fighting for the rights of a one hundred year old pensioner who was banned from having a clabber in the street.

"What's good for one centenarian was good for all," was his argument. Wee Malky spent the first two hours in the European court trying to explain that he *was* speaking English. His pleadings were in vain and the case was thrown out although many said it was because they couldn't understand him. Totally dejected Wee Malky wanted to throw himself out of the plane on his way back. But was talked out of it by the appearance of a stewardess with a double whisky

Friday morning and the noise of roaring engines mixed with loud voices made Sadie jump from bed. She hurried to the window and pulled back the curtain. The sight before her made her gasp. Two large yellow monsters stood there, ready for the attack. One tin-hatted man sat at the controls of the ball and chain vehicle an all around them were scores of placard waving people. Most of the messages supported the McPhatters.

Don't gie in! – Shame on Parliament – Smoking Kills – Read Oor Wullie every week in the Sunday Post.

One placard said *Sorry Folks* – held high by Tommy Sherman himself. Wee Malky lay drunk at his feet. Sir Murdo McWhachle stood with a huge grin on his face. His £300 teeth flashed in the sunlight.

He held a green flag aloft ready to bring down and signal the start of the massacre. Sadie could see the bulldozer drivers shifting in their seats and licking their lips. Like Formula One drivers, ready and itching for the off.

Hector McNab was circumnavigating the building giving it a final check.

Sir Murdo's grin stretched even wider. He had demanded that Sadie and Harry *leave these premises at once* – in his quietest whisper. Norman was not at home. He was auditioning for the Pantheon Club.

Murdo's arm came down quckly and the bulldozers revved up. Harry and Sadie lifted their packed suitcases after clearing away the barricade from the door. Harry opened the door and they both stood and let their eyes sweep round the room. Sadie sniffed and choked.

As they went to step out into the close the roaring noise of the bulldozers suddenly stopped. Only the angry voices of the placard wavers could be heard – *Away an' bile yer heid! – MSP'S . . . Merchant's of Stupid Patter – C'mon, Get aff – Brooke Bond Tea.*

Sadie and Harry peered out of the window. Sir Murdo McWhachle and Hector McNab were in deep conversation. Murdo's smile had vanished and the street was much darker.

Hector was holding something and pointing it out to Murdo, whose face was growing longer by the second.

"Ah wonder whit's up?" Sadie said. Harry did not reply.

Hector McNab turned away from his altercation with Sir Murdo and stormed up the close. The McPhatter's door was still wide open and Hector barged in.

"Youse two must be the jammiest pair in Glesca," Hector cried.

"Oh, aye, we've just won the lottery," Sadie said sarcastically.

"Naw, no' the lottery, hen," Hector said, "the keys o' yer hoose back. Put yer cases doon ye're no' goin' anywhere."

"Whit – whi – whi – dae ye mean?" Sadie stammered, excitement in her voice.

"Look," Hector McNab said, handing Sadie a plaque.

"Whit is it?" Sadie said, her hand shaking.

"It's a commerative plaque," Hector said, "Ah came across it when Ah was gein' the buildin' a final examination. It wis lyin' on the grun – er – ground, obviously hivin' fell off the wa'. I don't know how Ah missed it before."

"Whit does it say?" Sadie asked trembling.

"Read it," Hector said.

Sadie cleared her throat and began to read:

> *In this building on May the nineth,*
> *in the year of Our Lord*
> *eighteen hundred and sixty, was born*
> JAMES M BARRIE,
> *Writer and Playwright*

"Ah thought Barrie was born in Kirriemuir?" Sadie said. "Whit does it mean?"

"It means mair than ma life's worth for to proceed wi' the demolition of this building. This will become a listed building – a famous structure preserved for posterity – a shrine to a great Scot. Ah canny see how Ah missed that plaque during ma minute examinations. Ah'm sure Ah looked at that particular coarner wa' just last week,."

"Ye – ye mean we can stey?" Sadie was beside gerself with joy.

"Oh aye, hen. Ye've won," Hector was gallant in defeat.

"Whit aboot the dampness," Sadie said.

"That'll be taken care of," Hector said. "In fact the whole buildin' will be renovated. And the tenants who left wull be offered their hoo – er – houses back if they should wish for to return."

"Oh, Harry!" Sadie said, kissing her husband on the cheek.

Harry smiled. "It was meant to be – you findin' that plaque," he said. "Tell me, Mr McNab, whit's it made of?"

Hector turned the plaque over a couple of times examining it closely. He shrugged, "Looks like bronze tae me," he said. "Aye – bronze."

Sadie smiled and looked at Harry.

"Imagine that!" she said.

"Aye, just imagine," Harry smiled.

Hector shook hands and left. Sadie watched him as he and Sir Murdo walked down the street arguing. The bulldozers revved up louder, turned and rumbled away into the distance, vanishing round the corner. All was quiet again in Glenvernon Street. Sadie threw up the window and propped a cushion on the sill, She knelt on a chair and leaned out of the window. It was like old times. A wee girl appeared and drew *beds* on the pavement and began to play peever.

"No' up watchin' the telly, hen?" Sadie said.

The wee girl shook her head. "Naw," she said,"Ah love playin' peever. Did you ever play peever, missus?"

"Oh, aye hen," Sadie said, " Ah played peever a long time ago." Suddenly Erchie the barman, came running up from around the corner. He was puffing and panting and stopped when he saw Sadie at the window.

"Aw Ah'm wabbit!" he said. "Is Harry in?"

"Aye, away in," Sadie said, calling on Harry.

"We caught a pickpocket in the pub and when we searched him we found this." Erchie held up a wallet.

"Ma wallet!" Harry cried through the window. "C'mon in Erchie"

Norman came hurrying down the street all excited. "Hey, Mammy," he hollered, "Ah got the part in their new musical"

"Good for you, son," Sadie said. "Whit is it , *Rose Marie*?"

"Naw," Norman said, "*Les Miserables*. It means Ah'll be steyin' ower a few mair weeks."

"Whit aboot yer wife, Pokachips, or whatever her name is?"

"Oh, she'll be oot trappin'," Norman said.

"Oh, she's a trapper, eh?" Harry said,

"We're plagued wi' mice," Norman said.

"Well, come away in son, we've really got somethin' tae celebrate noo," Sadie said.

Harry poured out four glasses of what was left of Abdul's whisky and they raised their glasses.

"Aye, well, forty years," Sadie said, trying not to weep, "Forty wonderful years. These four walls have seen joy and love. Aye, and they've seen tears, tae. Ah raise ma gless tae the great loves o' ma life – and Ah thank God for shinin' his face doon on me," Sadie raised her glass higher. "Tae ma Harry who even yet can still surprise me. An tae Norman and Maggie and Norman's wife and to J.M. Barrie and his wonderful plaque – right, Harry?"

Harry smiled. "Ah telt ye things would work oot," he said a wry smile on his lips. "But have ye no' forgot tae toast the real wan we've loved a' these years?" he added.

"Of course Ah hivnae" Sadie, raising her glass even higher. "Tae *OOR HOOSE*," she said proudly.

LINDSAY PUBLICATIONS

PO BOX 812 GLASGOW G14 9NP
TEL/FAX 0141 569 6060
ISBN Prefix 1 898169

1 898169 00 4	*Scottish Home Baking*	Paterson	£4.95
03 9	*Scottish Home Cooking*	Paterson	£4.95
01 2	*Highland Dancing*	SOBHD	£10.00
08 X	*Glasgow's River*	Osborne	£9.99
06 3	*Homecraft*		£3.50
05 5	*Taste of Scotland*	Fitzgibbon	£8.99
10 1	*The Surgeon's Apprentice*	Young	£4.99
07 1	*Robert Burns*	Paterson	£4.50
12 8	*Savour of Scotland*	Morrison	£9.99
09 8	*Savour of Ireland*	Morrison	£9.99
11 X	*Lines Around the City*	Harvie	£10.99
13 6	*Still a Bigot*	Barclay	£4.99
14 4	*Happy Landings*	Barclay	£4.99
15 2	*Twisted Knickers & Stolen Scones*	Nicoll	£9.99
16 0	*Away with the Ferries*	Craig	£9.99
17 9	*Will I be Called an Author?*	Stuart	£7.99
23 3	*A Wheen O'Blethers*	Gray	£8.99
19 5	*Topsy & Tim aig an Dotair*	Adamson	£4.99
18 7	*T & T aig an Fhiaclair*	Adamson	£4.99
21 7	*T & T agus na Polis*	Adamson	£4.99
20 9	*T & T agus na Smaladairean*	Adamson	£4.99
24 1	*Oot the Windae*	Reilly	£6.99
22 5	*Laughing Matters*	Herron	£8.99
25.X	*Oor Hoose*	Barclay	£4.99